Lernthriller Englisch

MASSACRE UNITED

Jennifer Pickett

compact

Weitere Informationen zu Compact Lernthrillern finden Sie am Ende des Buches und unter www.lernkrimi.de.

Baierbrunner Straße 27, 81379 München
Ausgabe 2013

Chefredaktion: Dr. Matthias Feldbaum
Redaktion: Helga Aichele
Fachkorrektur: Nathalie Russell
Produktion: Frank Speicher
Titelabbildung: shutterstock.com: Tomasz Bidermann
Lernkrimi-Logo: Carsten Abelbeck
Gestaltung: EKH Werbeagentur München GbR, textum GmbH
Umschlaggestaltung: EKH Werbeagentur München GbR, Hartmut Baier

ISBN 978-3-8174-9319-7
381749319/1

www.compactverlag.de, www.lernkrimi.de

VORWORT

Liebe Leserin, lieber Leser,

mitreißend und unheimlich spannend – die Compact Lernthriller mit ihrer Kombination aus fesselnder Lektüre und didaktischem Übungsanteil eignen sich hervorragend, um breite Sprachkompetenzen in der Fremdsprache zu erwerben. Der Lerner wird dabei durch die atemberaubende Handlung, das angemessene Sprachniveau und den stetig ansteigenden Schwierigkeitsgrad der Übungen gefördert und motiviert. Ein ausführlicher Abschlusstest ermöglicht das Wiederholen und Festigen des Gelernten. In einem alphabetischen Glossar am Ende des Buches sind noch einmal übersichtlich alle Vokabeln zum Nachschlagen aufgelistet.

So lernen Sie mit Compact Lernlektüren:

- **Mit Begeisterung lernen:** Die packende Handlung motiviert Sie beim Lesen des englischen Originaltextes.
- **Wissen intensivieren und erweitern:** Durch die Kombination aus didaktisierter Lektüre und textbezogenen Übungen testen und trainieren Sie Ihre Sprachkenntnisse effektiv. Vokabelangaben auf jeder Seite unterstützen Sie beim Lesen.
- **Systematisch lernen:** Knüpfen Sie an Ihr individuelles Sprachniveau an und setzen Sie eigene Lernziele – linear im Schwierigkeitsgrad ansteigend oder mit punktuellen Schwerpunkten von Grundwortschatz bis Hörverstehen.
- **Unabhängig sein:** Lernen Sie ganz individuell – wo und wann Sie wollen.

Viel Spaß beim **spannend Englisch lernen**
wünscht Ihnen

Prof. Dr. Christiane Neveling
Didaktik der romanischen Sprachen, Universität Leipzig

INHALT

ZU DIESEM BUCH

Eine Reihe brutaler Morde hält Manchester in Atem. Ist es Zufall, dass mehrere der Opfer Fans des Clubs Manchester United waren? Oder haben die Morde etwas mit einem Massaker in den Neunzigerjahren zu tun?
Fußballreporter Rob Anderson bringt die Polizei auf eine neue Spur und wird dadurch tiefer in den Fall verwickelt, als ihm lieb ist. Als Rob eines Nachts verfolgt wird, kommt ihm ein schrecklicher Gedanke: Ist er etwa das nächste Opfer des gnadenlosen Killers?

Die Ereignisse und die handelnden Personen in diesem Buch sind frei erfunden. Etwaige Ähnlichkeiten mit tatsächlichen Ereignissen oder lebenden Personen wären rein zufällig und unbeabsichtigt.

1 MATCH DAY

The crowd cheered as the ball flew into the back of the net. The sound echoed around the stadium as thousands of Manchester United fans jumped to their feet. The striker lifted his shirt over his head and ran down the pitch, his arms spread wide in celebration.

"YES!" shouted Rob and hugged his friend Dave in joy.

"Go team!"

The game was nearing half-time, and Manchester United was leading by two goals to one in the premier league afternoon match. The opposition team were also playing well, but they were beginning to look tired. As usual Old Trafford, Manchester United's home stadium, was full. The early October sun was bright and the terraces of the stadium were a sea of red and white.

to cheer	jubeln
stadium	Stadion
striker	Stürmer
pitch	Spielfeld, Platz
defender	Verteidiger
to yell	brüllen, schreien

Fernando, Manchester United's expensive new player, had the ball again and was racing down the pitch. He dribbled the ball round the defenders, his red shirt standing out against the green grass. He ran past another player and the crowd grew more excited.

"Come on, come on!" yelled Dave. "Shoot!"

Fernando got the ball round a second defender. The ball seemed

glued	festgeklebt
to roar	brüllen, (auf)heulen
to groan	(auf)stöhnen
stand	Zuschauertribüne
benefit	Vorteil, Vorzug
to tease	necken, aufziehen

to be **glued** to his feet. He passed another player and the crowd **roared**.
"Shoot!"
The ball flew through the air and the goal keeper stretched out his arms. For one glorious moment it seemed as if the ball would get past him. Then the goal keeper's fingers connected with the ball and he pushed it away.
The crowd **groaned**.

Exercise 1: Match-up. Welche der folgenden Wortteile gehören zusammen? Ordnen Sie zu!

1. ☐ opposition	a) keeper
2. ☐ goal	b) league
3. ☐ premier	c) Trafford
4. ☐ Old	d) team

From their position in the **stands**, Rob and Dave had a fantastic view of the pitch. As Rob often reminded his friend, there were some **benefits** to being a journalist for *Fans United*. As a regular writer for the largest unofficial Manchester United fan magazine, 'mega fan' Rob Anderson was often invited to special events at the club. The brilliant seats also came with the job.
"I hope you're taking notes," **teased** Dave.
"What?" said Rob, not taking his eyes from the pitch.

"You know, for the magazine..."

"Hmm...oh come on, **ref**!" shouted Rob.

"How did you get so lucky? I mean, being paid to watch football!"

↯ ref (referee)	↯ Schiri
cheeky	frech, unverschämt
proper	anständig, richtig
tackle	Angriff, Tackling

Rob laughed, "It must be my charming smile!"

"Yeah, right."

Rob was a good-looking man, and they both knew it. His charm and his **cheeky** smile meant they were never short of female company. It had also gotten them into trouble several times when they were younger.

Rob had been coming to Old Trafford ever since he was a little boy. His dad had brought him to his first match. For Rob, walking out of the tunnels onto the stands was still as exciting as that first time. The noise of the crowd, the referee's whistle, and the bright red of the team colours still made his heart beat faster.

"Susan didn't want to come?" asked Dave.

Rob gave his friend a look. "When has Susan ever wanted to go to a football match?"

"She still wants you to get a '**proper**' job then?" laughed Dave.

"Hrmph! (i)"

The opposition's striker made a desperate **tackle** which left a Manchester United player on the ground. Rob and Dave joined the crowd as a shout went around the stadium.

"Oi, Referee!"

Lautmalerische Ausrufe unterscheiden sich zwischen den Sprachen. Hier sind einige aus dem Text:

Hrmph. [he/rumpf]	Räuspern, drückt Ärger oder Beleidigtsein aus, aber mit einem Hauch von Humor
Oi!	He! (um Aufmerksamkeit zu erregen, etw. derb)
Yep.	Zustimmung (= 'Yes')
Erm.	Hmmm.
Whoops(ie)! [whups]	Uups!

An hour later, the noise hit them as soon as they opened the heavy pub doors. It was full of football fans celebrating the victory and reliving the game.

Exercise 2: Adjectives. Lesen Sie weiter und unterstreichen Sie alle sechs Adjektive im folgenden Absatz!

It was tradition for Rob and Dave to go to the pub nearest the ground after the match. It was old, shabby and always busy, but it had a great atmosphere. Today was no exception. Red football shirts and scarves were everywhere.

Rob was lucky and managed to get them seats at a table near the door while Dave went to the bar. The pub was warm with so many people packed in. Rob took off his hat and coat. His curly brown hair stood up in all directions.
Dave came back to the table with their drinks, a look of intense concentration on his face as he tried to get the full pint glasses through the lively crowd without spilling beer all over himself!
"Cheers," said Dave as they settled into their seats.
They could just see the television on the wall. It was playing highlights of the match.
"Are you going to the match next week?" asked Rob.
Dave laughed. "Silly question!"
The football highlights had finished and the news came on.

to relive	(im Geiste) noch einmal erleben
pint	Pint (0,568 l)
cheers	Prost

"I'll be covering it for the magazine. I have to interview the club chairman after the match. I'll be watching from the manager's box," continued Rob.

"You're so lucky!" moaned Dave. "The view will be amazing!"

"Yes. I can bring a friend, too. Do you want to join me?"

"Erm…yes!"

"Ha ha ha." Rob laughed.

Dave opened the packets of peanuts and crisps he'd bought at the bar. He put them on the table in from of them so that Rob could help himself. As the two men sat drinking their beers, for a moment it was suddenly quieter in the pub and they could hear the television over the sound of people talking.

chairman	Vorsitzender
to moan	stöhnen
crisps *pl*	Kartoffelchips
victim	Opfer
serial killer	Serienmörder
to stab to death	erstechen
clue	Hinweis
bouncer	Türsteher

"…Another victim of the Manchester serial killer has been found. A man in his fifties was found stabbed to death in his own home. Again the police have no clues. They are asking people to be careful. If you have any information, please call this number…"

Suddenly there was a crash from the direction of the bar. It was followed by loud, angry voices.

"Oh, here we go," said Dave. "There's always someone ready to cause trouble after a match."

"Well, they won't be causing it for long," replied Rob and nodded towards the front of the pub.

Two huge bouncers had left their places by the door and were pushing their way through the crowd.

As the crowd moved aside, Rob and Dave could see the two men arguing at the bar. The shouting had now moved on to pushing.

to throw the first punch	den ersten Schlag austeilen
fool	Idiot
opponent	Gegner, Widersacher
ϟ mate	ϟ Kumpel
to chuckle	kichern
odd	*hier:* einzeln, gelegentlich
editor	Redakteur
column	Kolumne
ϟ The cheek!	So eine Frechheit!
ϟ to fancy sth.	auf etw. Lust haben, etw. wollen

It was only a matter of time before someone **threw the first punch**.

"I don't believe it," groaned Rob as he recognized one of the men. "That's James Parker. We work together. He's a complete **fool**!"

The bouncers reached James and his **opponent** and began marching them towards the doors of the pub. But James wasn't going to leave quietly. He was a big man with black hair and angry, dark eyes behind his glasses. He was still shouting back as the bouncers pushed him forwards.

"He started it! That idiot knocked over my drink."

"Whatever, **mate**!" said the other man.

Rob hid behind Dave as the bouncers pushed the two fighters past them.

"He's not a friend of yours, then?" **chuckled** Dave.

"You must be joking!" replied Rob. "The man is an idiot. He's loud and arrogant and thinks he's better than everyone else! He writes the **odd** article for the magazine when the **editor** can't find anyone better. However, his main job is to write the 'Fan of the Week' **column**."

"The what?"

"You know the kind of thing. Fans write in with a photograph, some basic information and a reason why they should be 'fan of the week'. If they are chosen, James puts them in his column," Rob explained. "He thinks this makes him a brilliant journalist."

Dave raised his eyebrows questioningly.
"Long story," said Rob, "but James likes to tell the rest of us journalists just what we are doing wrong."
"The cheek!" teased Dave.
Rob laughed. "Fancy another pint?"

Exercise 3: Contracted forms. Verwenden Sie Kurzformen, um die Sätze neu zu schreiben!

1. "Well, they will not ________________ be causing it for long."
2. "I do not ________________ believe it."
3. That is ________________ James Parker.
4. You are ________________ so lucky!
5. But James was not ________________ going to leave quietly.
6. When the editor can not ________________ find anyone better.

"...And the second goal was amazing!" Rob went on. "You should have seen the way Fernando kicked the ball past the goal keeper. I've never seen a goal like it!"
"Uh huh," said Susan, not taking her eyes off the television screen.
Her blonde hair was tied back in a ponytail. She was twenty-six, so a couple of years younger than Rob. Not that it was obvi-

ous. Their friends always joked that Susan was the **sensible** one. Tonight she was relaxing in black leggings and a loose purple jumper.

As usual on a Saturday night, she was pretending to listen to Rob describing that afternoon's match. The journey across Manchester from Trafford in the west to their flat in Didsbury in the south of the city hadn't reduced his enthusiasm at all.

Exercise 4: Hidden words. Finden Sie im Gitternetz zehn Wörter zum Thema Fußball!

M	A	N	A	G	E	R	J	Y	T
A	G	F	D	N	E	T	O	D	S
T	O	R	W	M	S	G	N	E	T
C	A	D	H	A	L	R	T	F	R
H	L	F	I	P	T	E	O	E	I
W	K	B	S	U	M	F	G	N	K
E	E	Q	T	O	I	E	H	D	E
J	E	K	L	A	C	R	K	E	R
I	P	C	E	M	V	E	Z	R	L
C	E	P	L	A	Y	E	R	N	B
B	R	S	T	A	D	I	U	M	H

"The referee was **biased**, of course," Rob said.

"Yep."

Susan's programme [i] finished and the credits began to play. She sat back on the sofa and put her feet on Rob's lap. He stroked them absent-mindedly.

" we should have had a free kick after half-time, of course. I don't know how the referee didn't see it!'

Achtung, nicht verwechseln: **programme** (US: **program**) heißt „Sendung". Das deutsche „Programm" wird dagegen mit **channel** (Kanal) übersetzt. Um herauszufinden, was im TV läuft, schaut man in die **TV listings** (Fernsehprogramm). **Zapping** heißt auch **channel hopping.**

Susan sighed and sat up. The left-overs from their Chinese takeaway covered the table. She began to tidy up.

"Have you finished with that, sweetheart?" she asked, taking Rob's dirty plate away.

"Yes, thanks. Anyway, Fernando was brilliant. It's only his first season with the club and he's scored four goals already."

"Uh huh," replied Susan as she walked into the kitchen.

"Four goals!"

Susan turned on the taps in the sink to do the washing up.

"Amazing," she called sarcastically over the noise.

"Unbelievable!" Rob suddenly shouted angrily.

"Pardon?"

Susan came back into the room, alarmed by the anger in Rob's voice. She found him staring at the television. The news reporter looked very serious as he read the report.

"...It has been confirmed that no further action will be taken in the case of Jared Cook. Mr Cook

sensible	vernünftig
biased	*hier*: parteiisch
credits *pl*	*hier*: Abspann
absent-mindedly	geistesabwesend
tap	Wasserhahn
to confirm	bestätigen
case	Fall

was the only person jailed for the Manchester United coach massacre in 1996. After 16 years in prison, Mr Cook was released when a judge found there were problems with his original trial. Mr Cook has now been free for five months."

"What's this?" asked Susan. "Why has it upset you so much?"

"This man killed ten people. Then they let him out of prison just because a policeman made a mistake years ago!"

to jail	inhaftieren, einsperren
to release	freilassen
trial	Gerichtsverfahren
solicitor	Anwalt
evidence	Beweis(e)
to provide	liefern, bereitstellen
gunman	Bewaffneter
justice	Gerechtigkeit
to pace	auf und ab gehen

"You don't think he is innocent?"

"Not at all! He was lucky that his solicitor found a problem with some of the evidence. But that doesn't mean he is innocent. Everyone knows he's guilty, even the police."

"But surely if they let him go…?"

"Jared Cook is evil, Susan. He used a machine gun on a coach full of innocent people just to kill one man."

The news reporter continued. "…The policeman who provided the problem evidence has not been identified. The second gunman has never been found. In all the years since the massacre, Jared Cook has never spoken about that day. It looks as if the victims of the Manchester United coach massacre will never get justice."

The news reporter moved on to other stories. Rob stood up and paced the room. He was so angry.

"No one is going to pay for what happened that day. It's not right!"

to be supposed to do sth.	etw. tun sollen
file	Akte
anniversary	Jahrestag
awful	furchtbar, schrecklich

"What happened, Rob?" asked Susan. "The shooting was long before I moved to Manchester and I don't remember the case."

Rob sat down on the sofa and put his head in his hands. Susan was alarmed by his reaction. She sat next to him and wrapped her arms around his shoulders.

"I was supposed to be at the match that day. My dad was going to take me, but I was sick so we stayed at home. The first time we heard about the shooting was on the television."

Exercise 5: Irregular verbs. Ergänzen Sie Simple Past und Past Participle der folgenden unregelmäßigen Verben!

1. hear ____________ ____________
2. take ____________ ____________
3. go ____________ ____________
4. know ____________ ____________
5. be ____________ ____________

Rob got up abruptly and left the room. He was back in a minute with a thick file. He opened it and handed Susan a piece of paper. "This is an article I wrote for the fifteenth anniversary of the massacre. I won a prize for it." He smiled sadly. "It was strange to get a prize for writing about something so awful."

Susan began to read out loud. "The 23rd March 1996 is known as one of the worst days in the history of Manchester United Football Club. It was a day when drugs and gangs met football with terrible results. It had been a fantastic match at Old Trafford. Manchester United had beaten their bitter rivals Liverpool United by two goals to one. Thousands of happy fans were celebrating as they started to leave the stadium to go home."

treat	*hier*: Aufmerksamkeit, Geschenk
to glance	blicken
to force	zwingen
balaclava	Sturmhaube
grim	grimmig, finster
to shatter	zerbrechen, zersplittern

"I was so jealous," added Rob. "I was watching the match on the television and I really wanted to be there."
Susan carried on reading. "In the car park, a group of fans got onto their coach for their journey home. All the conversations were about the match and their team's victory. None of them knew that Michael Sullivan, one of Manchester's most dangerous gangsters, was also on the coach. Sullivan (a life-long Manchester United fan) had brought his twelve-year-old son Jeremy to the match. It was a special treat to celebrate Sullivan's recent release from jail."
Susan glanced at Rob. "This was all because of one man?"
He nodded. "That is the theory."
"...The coach moved slowly through the crowds. As it came close to the gates, the number of fans crossing the car park forced it to stop. Suddenly there was a loud noise at the front of the coach. Two men wearing black balaclavas and carrying machine guns forced open the coach doors and climbed onto the vehicle. The coach driver was shot in the leg as he tried to start the engine.

Michael Sullivan realized what was happening. He stood up and pulled out his own gun."

Exercise 6: True or false? Welche Aussagen sind korrekt? Markieren Sie mit richtig ✔ oder falsch – !

1. Rob wrote the article for the tenth anniversary of the coach massacre. ☐
2. Michael Sullivan had recently been released from prison. ☐
3. The shooting occurred after the football match had finished. ☐
4. Manchester United lost the match on the 23rd March 1996. ☐
5. Michael Sullivan took his daughter to watch the game. ☐

Susan glanced at Rob again. His face was grim.
"The gunfight that followed lasted for less than a minute, but the results will last for generations. Fathers threw themselves over their children to try and protect them…" Susan swallowed. "Rob, this is awful."
"…The coach windows were shattered by bullets. Blood covered the seats and floor. Seven people died on the coach and another in an ambulance. Three more died in hospital over the next two days. The youngest victim was just six years old. His grandfather had taken him to see his first ever football match."

Exercise 7: Missing words. Lesen Sie weiter und setzen Sie die angegebenen Begriffe richtig ein!

gun | Minister | survived | instantly | country

"Sullivan was shot in the head and died **1.** ______.
His son Jeremy was seriously **injured** but **2.** ______.
He has since become a **campaigner** against **3.** ______ crime. As the Prime **4.** ______ John Major said at the time, 'This was not only a sad day for Manchester United but for the whole **5.** ______'. The 23rd March 1996 is remembered as one of the bloodiest moments in the history of Manchester's gang wars."

They sat in silence for a few moments, thinking about the massacre. It seemed crazy that something so terrible had happened in the city they lived in. Finally Susan squeezed his hand before standing up. She collected the last glasses from the table and went back to the kitchen. She knew that Rob needed some space to calm down. The news report had really upset him. After a while he decided to turn on his computer and play his football manager game. The game **distracted** him enough that the news report finally slipped from his mind.

Not far away, the killer **shifted his weight** from foot to foot. The long wait in the cold had made his legs go stiff. It would all be worth it, though. **Preparation** was the secret. It was why he had managed to escape the police so far. He watched and he waited. It wasn't time to strike until he knew his victim's routine so well that he imagined he knew what they were thinking.

He snorted, "Victims!"

They were all guilty, every one of them. And they were all going to pay.

In the shadows of his hiding place, no one could see the killer. People walking down the street passed just feet away from him. He almost wondered how they couldn't feel him there, feel his hate, his anger. At times it was so powerful he felt as if it were bursting from his body.

injured	verletzt
campaigner	Aktivist, Kämpfer
to distract	ablenken
to shift one's weight	sein Gewicht verlagern
preparation	Vorbereitung
to strike	zuschlagen, angreifen
to snort	schnauben, prusten
to burst	bersten, herausbrechen
cosy	heimelig, gemütlich
target	Ziel

Exercise 8: Verb forms. Lesen Sie weiter und unterstreichen Sie die richtige Verbform!

From where he stood, the killer could **1.** seen / see straight across the road to the flat. He **2.** had seen / see his man **3.** came / come home. He had enjoyed **4.** imagined / imagining the cosy scene inside. Then he had seen his target briefly once again when he came to the window to close the curtains. Now the killer **5.** watched / watches as the lights in the flat were **6.** turned / turning off one by one.

physical	körperlich
to overwhelm	überwältigen, überschwemmen
to mutter	murmeln
to clench one's fists	die Fäuste ballen
to blend into sth.	verschmelzen mit

His anger rose inside him again. It was such a physical thing. Sometimes it felt like a wave that would overwhelm him.

"No! Not yet," he muttered to himself, his fists clenched tightly by his sides. "It's not the right time."

But when that time came, he was going to make that man pay. With one last look at the flat, the killer marched off into the night, his black clothing blending into the darkness.

2 AN UNFORTUNATE ENCOUNTER

"Ah, that's better."

Greg settled down in his armchair and took a long drink from his can of beer, which he had balanced on his belly. This Saturday was much like every other in the football season. Football, beer, peace and quiet! The students next door were probably still asleep. They wouldn't have got away with that when he was young, thought Greg. Fallowfield, where he lived, was a fairly nice area popular with students.

It had been a long week. Most days Greg liked being a taxi driver. He could choose the hours he worked and he was his own boss. However, some of his passengers could be hard work. Yesterday he'd had an old lady who couldn't find her house keys, and then he'd given a lift to two drunk and very loud men. Nonetheless, it was more reliable than some of the dodgier things he used to do.

Greg chuckled to himself. "I'm a bit old for all that now!"

encounter	Begegnung
to settle down	es sich bequem machen
to get away with sth.	mit etw. durchkommen
reliable	verlässlich
ϟ dodgy	zweifelhaft, riskant

"...Manchester United will need to try something new for the rest of the match," said the TV in the corner of his living room, in-

fortnight	vierzehn Tage
to burp	rülpsen
divorce	Scheidung
nagging	nörgelnd
to wobble	schwanken, wackeln
muffled	gedämpft

terrupting Greg's thoughts. "They have been struggling here today. This match has been nothing like the four-goal triumph a fortnight ago. We'll have to see if the manager's half-time talk will make a difference..."

The commentators finished talking and the cameras switched to a view of the inside of the stadium. The players were walking back on to the pitch. It was raining heavily but the football ground was still full of supporters. The referee blew his whistle and the second half started.

Exercise 9: Unscramble. **Bringen Sie die Buchstaben in die richtige Reihenfolge!**

1. serepssagn ______________________
2. hiarramc ______________________
3. erbailel ______________________
4. tteirrunp ______________________
5. urtonecen ______________________
6. ifgnotrht ______________________

Greg burped loudly. "Come on, United!"

The divorce from Tracey had been difficult, but if Greg was honest, sometimes living alone had its benefits. Like now for

example, there was no nagging wife and no noisy kids wanting attention. He could watch the match, drink his beer and eat whatever junk food he wanted. He could put his feet up on the coffee table and watch the football with no interruptions.
The game continued. The collection of empty beer cans at Greg's feet grew.

Exercise 10: Fill in the verb. Lesen Sie weiter und setzen Sie die Verben passend ein!

runs | passes | is looking | approaches | were expecting

"...Now this is the Manchester United we **1.** ______ ! Fernando **2.** ______ to Griggs. Griggs **3.** ______ down the pitch. He **4.** ______ for space. He sees it! He passes to Flett. Flett **5.** ______ the goal..."

The door bell rang. Greg ignored it.
"...He is tackled by Turner and loses the ball. Griggs chases him down..."
The door bell rang again. With a sigh, Greg stood up. He wobbled slightly from the beer. The door bell rang again. Whoever was at the door held his finger on the button.
"I'm coming, I'm coming!" Greg yelled. "Who is it?"
"A parcel for you." The voice from the other side of the door was muffled.

blurred	verschwommen
form	Formular
to collapse	zusammen-brechen
blade	Klinge
terrified	total verängstigt
sinister	unheilvoll, unheimlich

"I'm not expecting anything."

Greg was standing in his hallway. He could see the television through the doorway to the living room.

"It's got your name on the label, mate," replied the voice.

There was a loud cheer from the television. Greg muttered in frustration. The visitor at the door was not going to go away. Greg could just see a blurred figure through the glass in the front door. A discussion through the door was just wasting time. Greg needed to get the parcel so he could get back to watching the game.

"Hang on a moment."

Greg unlocked the door. The delivery man gave him a wide smile. "Alright, mate. It's heavy," he said, gesturing to the large box in his arms. "I'll bring it in for you."

Greg led the way down the hall. The delivery man followed him and put the box down at the bottom of the stairs.

"Can I just get you to sign this, please?" The delivery man reached into his jacket to get his form.

"Yeah sure."

Greg had his eyes back on the television. Suddenly he saw a flash of metal out of the corner of his eye. It was followed by a terrible, burning pain. Greg collapsed against the door frame. The delivery man pulled the blade out of Greg's shoulder with a grunt. Greg's eyes widened in fear as the knife arched towards him again. Terrified, he dived through the door of the living room. He collided with the coffee table which smashed. He landed on the carpet in the centre of the room. The delivery man followed him, a sinister smile on his face.

Exercise 11: Adjective match-up. **Ordnen Sie die Gegenteile zu!**

1. ☐ heavy — a) narrow
2. ☐ wide — b) light
3. ☐ blurred — c) quiet
4. ☐ sinister — d) clear
5. ☐ loud — e) nice

"Who are you?" panted Greg in terror and pain.
The delivery man smiled. "You don't recognize me?"
Greg shook his head. His heart was pounding in his chest. His blood was covering his shirt and he was in agony. It was hard to think clearly.
"Maybe this will help you remember?"
The man strode across the room, the knife raised. Greg was not going to go down without a fight. He pulled himself up on the arm of the sofa and launched himself at the delivery man. His fingers struggled for a grip on the man's smooth coat. The knife stabbed into Greg's chest again and he screamed in pain. He kicked out with his legs and the two men fell to the ground. Chairs and shelves toppled over as the men wrestled. Greg could feel his strength leaving him.

to pant	keuchen, schnaufen
to pound	hämmern
agony	heftige Schmerzen
to stride	schreiten
to launch oneself at sb.	sich auf jmd. stürzen

to snarl	(wütend) knurren
to flinch	zusammenzucken
crime scene	Tatort
chart	Diagramm, Grafik

The man was on top of him now, snarling. Greg hit him as hard as he could, but his arms felt heavy. The attacker hardly flinched. The knife cut down into Greg's chest again and Greg moaned.

Sergeant Chris North pushed open the office door at Didsbury Police Station with his shoulder. His hands were full with two cups of coffee and packets of sandwiches. The large office was full of policemen and women busily doing their work. Sergeant North put the food and drinks down on the table in the centre of the room.
"Here we go, boss," he said.
His senior officer, Detective Inspector Archie McKay was standing next to the table and was staring at the crime scene photographs and charts on the wall. He didn't seem to have moved since Chris had left him twenty minutes ago. Sergeant North looked at his boss. DI McKay was in his forties. His hair was just beginning to turn grey at the sides. He usually had a smile on his face but today Chris thought he looked tired. This case was beginning to get to all of them. Sergeant North really liked his boss. DI McKay had looked after him since he joined the police force. Some of the senior officers didn't have time for the newer members of the team, but DI McKay was different. He understood that everyone had to learn. He expected his officers to work hard but he was always there to give advice.
DI McKay sighed and rubbed his eyes.
"Sir?" said Chris loudly. "You'd better drink it before it gets cold."
"Sorry, what?" said DI McKay, not taking his eyes from the wall.
"Your coffee, sir." Sergeant North gestured at the cups.

"Oh thanks, Chris," said DI McKay. He stood up and stretched.
"This case is a nightmare," added the senior policeman. "Three victims, no obvious connections and no clues." He shook his head.
"I've been a policeman for twenty years, and I have never seen a case like this before."
Sergeant North looked over to the photographs on the wall. The splashes of blood and the faces of the dead were very familiar to him.
"Let's start again," he suggested. "What do we know? Victim one, George Jenkins…"
Across the room, a phone rang. It was answered by one of the officers at the back. He listened carefully before calling DI McKay.
"Sir, they've found another body!"
The room went silent.

Exercise 12: Adjective or adverb? Ergänzen Sie die richtige Form!

1. The room was full of policemen and women busy ________________ doing their work.
2. Chris thought he looked tired ________________.
3. "Sir?" said Chris loud ________________.
4. "You'd better drink it before it gets cold ____________."
5. He listened careful ________________ before calling DI McKay.

A couple of miles away, Rob was on his way back home from Dave's house in Fallowfield. He was tired and hoarse from shouting at the match and looking forward to getting home. They'd taken the trams and then the bus together as far as Dave's house, then it was a brisk walk back to the flat. It was late afternoon and the autumn sun was starting to go down, which made the streets look rather gloomy.

"Okay, sweetheart. I'm on my way home now." Rob said goodbye to Susan and put his mobile phone back in his pocket.

Exercise 13: Translation. Lesen Sie weiter und übersetzen Sie die markierten Begriffe!

He **1.** gähnte ________________. The journey home after a match always took ages. Thousands of people all trying to get on the same trams to the **2.** Stadtzentrum ________________, then a bus south that seemed to **3.** anhalten ________________ every two minutes. Rob stepped down off the kerb in order to cross the road. The sound of approaching **4.** Sirenen ____________ made him step back hurriedly onto the **5.** Bürgersteig ________________.

He looked to his right and saw several blue and red flashing lights approaching. A police car raced past with its sirens blaring. It was followed by another and then another.

What's going on? thought Rob. It must be something big.
He checked again to see if it was safe to cross now. There was no traffic so he continued on his way. He put his headphones on and began to sing along.
"…a funny little thing, ooo oo ooh…"

hoarse	heiser
gloomy	düster, trostlos
kerb	Bordstein
to blare	heulen, dröhnen
to stagger	torkeln, wanken
homeless	obdachlos
shaken	erschüttert, aufgewühlt

Rob's stomach was rumbling. He knew Susan had a curry waiting for him at home. "…bop, bop, bop, hey baby."
He turned the corner of the street onto Wilmslow Road and a man ran straight into him. The force of the collision knocked Rob into the wall. The other man staggered backwards and nearly fell.
"Sorry, mate. Are you okay?" Rob stuttered, trying to catch his breath.
The man was holding his hand up against his body. He had what looked like blood on the front of his dirty coat. His hair was wild and his face was unshaven. He looked as if he could be homeless.
"Are you okay?" repeated Rob.
The man lifted his face and for one second his eyes met Rob's. He looked terrified and desperate. Then he was gone. Rob turned and watched him run down the street, holding his hand against his chest.
Rob slowly straightened himself up. He felt a bit shaken by the collision. His side ached from where he had hit the wall but otherwise he seemed to be okay. He started to walk home.
"Hang on a minute!" Rob's hand flew to his coat pocket in panic. His phone was still there. He checked his jeans pocket and

relief	Erleichterung
↯ fella	↯ Typ
dusk	Abenddämmerung
eager	begierig, eifrig
↯ chap	↯ Typ, Kerl
concerned	besorgt

sighed in **relief**: He still had his wallet.

Idiot, thought Rob. He should watch where he is going. Crazy-looking **fella**.

A couple of streets further on, Rob came across the police cars. The sirens were off but the flashing lights lit up the surrounding houses. The neighbours were all out on the street. They were standing in small groups in the **dusk** and looking nervously at the three policemen who were guarding a house. Another couple of police officers were going around talking to the watching crowd.

"What's going on?" Rob asked a middle-aged woman in an ugly brown anorak.

"Not sure, love."

She looked shocked but **eager** to talk. She leaned towards him secretively.

"Apparently they've found a body. The **chap** who lives there," she nodded at the house, "well, he's been murdered."

"Murdered?"

"That's what I heard. He was stabbed. Blood everywhere! The next-door neighbour heard screaming and crashes. Then she saw someone running, so she called the police. They found the body."

"Oh."

Rob was shocked. He was about ten minutes away from the flat he shared with Susan. The idea of a killer striking so close to home was a scary thought.

He walked on in a hurry. He just wanted to be indoors, and it seemed as if most people felt the same. The streets were empty and quiet.

Exercise 14: Sounds the same. Lesen Sie weiter und unterstreichen Sie die richtige Variante!

Suddenly Rob thought he heard footsteps running up behind him. He turned but there was no **1.** won / one there. His mind jumped **2.** to / too the homeless man. Why had he been running **3.** so / sew close to the scene of the murder? Rob knew the man had **4.** scene / seen his face. He looked around again, fearfully, but could **5.** see / sea nothing. Nevertheless, his heart was pounding in his chest. This was all **6.** to / too much!

Rob half ran the last few hundred yards home. Susan was surprised when he burst noisily into the flat, breathing heavily.
"Rob?" she called, coming out of the living room to meet him.
He dropped his keys and threw his arms around her. She was surprised but pleased.
She rubbed his back.
"Are you okay? What's happened?"
Rob buried his face in her shoulder-length blonde hair. Then he took a deep breath and explained. Susan's face changed from concerned to slightly amused.
"So, let me get this right," she said. "You think that you just collided with the serial killer. This killer, who has avoided the police for months, is actually a homeless man and you met him on your way home from the match."

"Well, I…," Rob muttered, rubbing the back of his neck.
"And this murdering homeless man then became invisible and followed you home?"
"Erm…"
Susan laughed. "You writers let your imaginations run away with you!"

The killer slammed the front door shut behind him and collapsed on the floor.
Damn, that was way too close! he thought, his heart racing. I really thought for a moment that they'd catch me and it would all be over before my job is finished. No, I can't let that happen.
"Never!" he shouted out loud, punching the floor and sobbing in a strange mix of anger and fear.
His journey home had been terrifying. He had hidden in doorways and taken extra turns to make sure no one was following him.

invisible	unsichtbar
imagination	Fantasie, Vorstellungskraft
close	*hier*: knapp
to sob	schluchzen
initial	erste(r,s), anfänglich

He leant his head back against the wall and tried to control his breathing. Control was everything. It had all gone so wrong tonight. He had to make sure there were no screams next time. And there would be a next time. He smiled through his tears into the darkness. Yes, there would definitely be a next time.
"They have to pay."
He couldn't believe how quickly the police had arrived…and then seeing Rob Anderson! What had he been doing there? Something would have to be done about that, and it would have to be done sooner than he'd originally planned.

Exercise 15: Word spiral. **Finden Sie die Begriffe in der Wortspirale!**

1	2	3	4	5	6	7	8
22	23	24	25	26	27	28	9
21	36	37	38	39	40	29	10
20	35	34	33	32	31	30	11
19	18	17	16	15	14	13	12

1-6: Wear these to keep your hands warm.
6-8: to cry uncontrollably
8-13: what goes in and out of your mouth
13-20: having nowhere to live
20-25: a shout of fear
25-32: *Fans United* is a ...
32-36: the opposite of full
36-40: older than a child but not an adult

Detective Inspector McKay nodded to the policeman guarding the front door. The first policemen at the house had secured the scene. DI McKay and Sergeant North had had to wait outside while the paramedics and the forensic team had done their initial work. Now Archie McKay pulled on his plastic gloves, took a deep breath and entered the house. Even after all these years, a murder scene could still make him feel ill. Archie had been to the scene of the other serial killer's victims. He knew what

to peer	spähen, schauen
to prevent sb. from doing sth.	jmd. daran hindern, etw. zu tun
stained	verfärbt, befleckt
ϟ tatty	schäbig, abgewetzt
to sparkle	glitzern
fierce	heftig, erbittert
to clear one's throat	sich räuspern
pattern	Muster, Schema

the inside of the house was going to look like.

"Chris?"

"In here, sir," came the voice from the living room.

DI McKay peered around the door. Sergeant North had gone in ahead of him and was now standing against the wall. In the far corner by an overturned television, two members of the crime scene investigation team were busy with the body on the floor, their white overalls preventing the DI from seeing much. So he took the opportunity to look around the room.

There was blood everywhere. It was splashed up the nicotine-stained walls and on the floor. The tatty, cheap furniture had been knocked over. Magazines, a spilt ashtray and a cracked photo frame lay on the floor. The glass from the photo frame sparkled in the worn, brown carpet.

"It seems there was a fierce struggle," said Sergeant North.

"Yes. This man fought back."

The crime scene investigators stood up and DI McKay cleared his throat.

"Good evening, gentlemen."

The taller of the two investigators removed his mask.

"Hello Archie."

DI McKay and Professor Frost had worked together for many years.

"There's not much new I can tell you, Archie. I'm certain this poor fella is a victim of our serial killer. It is the same pattern. There

is no sign of a break-in. Whoever the killer is, our victim let him into the house."
Archie sighed sadly. "Just like the others."
He approached the body. "Good grief!"
Archie had to cover his mouth and look away for a moment. The body was a mess. It was lying on its side and the victim's blue jeans were soaked in blood. His football shirt was torn at the back. The policemen could see many ragged stab wounds in the victim's skin. Professor Frost stood up and stretched his back.
"Time of death was about an hour ago," he said. "I think he was attacked first in the hall. That's where we found the first splashes of blood. The main struggle then took place in here. The weapon was some sort of large knife. You can see from the defence wounds on the victim's hands that he fought back, but that first stab wound had already done severe damage. He would have become weaker and weaker as he lost blood."
"What an awful way to die," said DI McKay.
Professor Frost began to methodically pack away his equipment.

ϟ Good grief!	Du meine Güte!
ragged	ausgefranst, zerrissen
severe	schwer, ernsthaft
swiftly	schnell
oppressive	(er)drückend

"Good luck, Archie," he said as he left the room. His assistant followed swiftly behind him.
The silence in the room was oppressive. The dead body was awful to look at.
"What do we know about the victim, Chris?" asked DI McKay quietly.
Sergeant North opened his notebook. "His name is Greg Summers. He's a taxi driver and lives alone. His neighbours don't

know much about him, but the lady next door thinks he spent some time in prison."

"Whatever he did, he didn't deserve this."

"Whoever did this was very angry," commented Chris. "It takes a lot of rage and hate to do this to someone."

"And it hasn't been long since we found the last victim," added DI McKay grimly. "The killer is speeding up; the time between the killings is getting shorter. We need to find him before he strikes again and we need to find him quickly."

Exercise 16: Opposites. Welche der folgenden Gegenteile gehören zusammen? Ordnen Sie zu!

1. ☐ speed up	a) gentle
2. ☐ dead	b) dry
3. ☐ soaked	c) strong
4. ☐ fierce	d) slow down
5. ☐ weak	e) alive

3 A TOO FAMILIAR FACE

"Good morning, Rob," a friendly voice greeted him.
Rob looked up from his computer screen. "Hi Cathy, did you have a nice weekend?"

fringe	*hier*: Pony
to blush	erröten
to wink	zwinkern
mischievously	verschmitzt, schelmisch

Exercise 17: Pronouns. Lesen Sie weiter und ergänzen Sie die fehlenden Pronomen!

She her him his He you

Cathy, the young, new office receptionist was smiling at **1.** ______ from the other side of **2.** ______ desk. **3.** ______ looked at him from under **4.** ______ long, dark **fringe** and **blushed**.
"Yes, thank you. I have some post for **5.** ______."
6. ______ **winked** at her **mischievously** and watched as her cheeks turned even pinker.

to capture	einfangen
to startle sb.	jmd. aufschrecken, jmd. erschrecken
incident	Vorfall, Zwischenfall
awkward	unangenehm, peinlich
notoriously	notorisch, bekannt für
private	*hier*: verschlossen, introvertiert
trolley	Rollwagen
stationery	Schreibwaren
ϟ to reckon	denken, glauben

"I, erm...," she stuttered.
"Thanks, Cathy."
She straightened up and hurried away. Rob watched her from his desk, admiring her long legs and nice bottom shown off by the tight skirt she was wearing.
"I'm only looking, darling," he told the photograph of Susan on his desk and returned to working on his article.
He needed to capture the atmosphere of Saturday's match. As Rob became absorbed in his article, the noise of the Monday morning office activities faded into the background.
"Hi Rob!"
James startled him a few minutes later. He hadn't heard James approaching his desk.
"Oh...Hi James."
Rob hadn't really spoken to James since the incident at the pub a fortnight ago. He had managed to avoid him when they'd both been in the office. There was an uncomfortable silence. Rob waited. He was sure James must want something. Finally, James cleared his throat.
"Did you see the match at the weekend, Rob?"
"Of course. It was a good result in the end."
"The second half was much better," agreed James.
There was another awkward pause.
"I hear the editor has asked you to interview Fernando next month."

"That's right," Rob replied.

It had taken a lot of time and hard work to arrange the interview. Fernando was notoriously private.

"Fernando is from Argentina, you know," James continued. "I spent quite some time there after university..."

So that was it! James was trying to steal Rob's interview. There was no way Rob was going to give up his interview for James. Will, the office assistant, was walking past slowly, pushing a trolley laden with stationery. A slim man, Will looked younger than his 23 years.

Rob called out to him in desperation. "Will!"

Will stopped next to Rob's desk and grinned. "Hi Rob, James. It was an exciting match on Saturday, eh?"

Rob was grateful to Will for changing the subject. The conversation moved on to debating what Adam Ferguson, the ManU manager, must have said to his team at half-time.

"I reckon the manager must have promised them a pay rise if they won," said Rob.

Exercise 18: Possessive apostrophes. Platzieren Sie die Apostrophe richtig, um die Genitivform zu bilden!

1. Robs computer ______________
2. the three mens editor ______________
3. the girls bottoms ______________
4. Rob and Wills conversation ______________
5. James laugh ______________

booming	dröhnend
balding	eine Glatze bekommen
preoccupied	besorgt, nachdenklich
memorabilia *pl*	Souvenirs
to head (back)	(zurück)eilen
puzzled	verwirrt
to run an article	einen Artikel bringen
to eavesdrop	(be)lauschen
lead	Spur, Hinweis

"Or a ticket home if they didn't," joked Will.

The number of foreign players in the Manchester United team was well known.

The editor's **booming** voice drew their attention to the front of the open-plan office.

"If you'd like to follow me, gentlemen..."

Kevin Skinner, their editor, was a short, **balding** man known for angry outbursts when he got stressed. Now he seemed to be quite **preoccupied** as he led his two serious-looking visitors towards his own office at the back.

"What's going on there?" wondered James.

The first visitor was middle-aged with greying hair and a pleasant but tired-looking face. The second visitor was much younger and taller. He was looking around with interest. His eyes opened wide as they walked past the football **memorabilia** on the office walls. He almost stopped to look, but then he seemed to remember where he was and hurried after the others.

"It looks pretty important, whatever it is," remarked Will as the editor's door shut firmly.

"Hmm," said James. "Speaking of important, I have work to do."

He **headed back** to his desk. Will rolled his eyes at Rob, who chuckled. Rob tried to focus on his article again, but his attention was still drawn to the editor's closed office door. Just what was going on in there?

Eventually the editor's door opened. Rob was surprised when Kevin led his two visitors across to his desk.

"Rob, let me introduce Detective Inspector McKay and Sergeant North from Greater Manchester Police."
Rob stood and shook the men's outstretched hands. He was puzzled but interested. What could the police want with him?
Kevin continued, "Rob, these gentlemen have asked if the magazine could run an article for them. I'd like you to write it."
"Let me explain," said DI McKay. "As you will know, a serial killer has been operating in Manchester over the past few months."
Rob nodded. Over DI McKay's shoulder he could see James by the photocopier, very obviously eavesdropping.
Typical, thought Rob and returned his attention to the policeman. "I've seen the stories on the news."

Exercise 19: Tricky tenses. Unterstreichen Sie die richtige Verbform!

1. Three people have been killed / were killed over the past few months.
2. At the moment Rob is interviewing / interviews Fernando.
3. We don't know where he strikes / will strike next.
4. Rob tried / was trying to write an article when the visitors arrived.
5. Yesterday the killer has struck / struck again.

"Good," said DI McKay and sat down on the edge of a neighbouring desk. "What you might not know is that we have very few leads. This killer is quite clever. His victims are all different, and

to predict sth.	etw. vorhersagen
to appeal for information	um Hinweise bitten
suspicious	verdächtig
to publish	veröffentlichen
sb.'s mind is whirling	jmd. schwirrt der Kopf
to shrug	die Schultern zucken
to pierce	durchbrechen

he doesn't seem to follow any specific pattern. So we cannot predict where he will strike next."

Rob nodded gravely. "I don't understand how I can help."

"The latest victim was a Mr Greg Summers, a taxi driver who lived alone. Mr Summers was watching football when he was killed," the Detective Inspector continued. "When his body was found, he was still wearing a Manchester United football shirt. Your magazine reaches thousands of people every week. We want to run an article in *Fans United* appealing for information. We want all your readers to think about anything suspicious they might have seen? Obviously we will read the article before it is published. Sergeant North will give you all the details you need. What do you think?"

"Of course I'll do it," said Rob without hesitation.

"Excellent," replied his editor. "Gentlemen, let me show you out."

Once the policemen had left, Rob sat down heavily at his desk. His mind was whirling. It was unlikely, but his article could lead to the capture of a serial killer. He looked up and met Will's eye. The young man was standing by the stationery cupboard. Will raised his eyebrows. Rob shrugged. He was surprised by the events of the past few minutes, too.

James's voice pierced the air. "Here, Will, come and look at this guy's name...Maximillian Fitzwilliam-Herbert-Smythe!" he laughed. "Ha ha ha! With a name like that, he can definitely be this week's 'fan of the week'. It's too ridiculous not to publish!"

Will rolled his eyes again at Rob before wandering over to James's desk. Rob tried to block out the sound of James's voice. He stared at the blank screen for a moment, wondering how you were supposed to start an article like this?

to buzz with sth.	erfüllt sein mit
massive	riesig
in awe	bewundernd
scornfully	verächtlich

The lift door closed and DI McKay and Sergeant North began their journey down to the ground floor. The detective glanced at his sergeant. Chris' eyes were sparkling and he was almost **buzzing with** excitement. He was a **massive** Manchester United[i] fan and Archie knew how excited he had been by this visit to the magazine offices. Given the seriousness of their visit, on the whole Chris had done a pretty good job of hiding his interest; now they were alone he couldn't hold it in any longer.

"Did you see the signed shirts, sir? They had one from David Peckham himself! Wow!"

"Wow indeed," said DI McKay dryly.

"And they had signed photographs of the whole team," commented Chris **in awe**.

"I'm a Newcastle United fan myself," added DI McKay.

"Well, I suppose someone has to be," the sergeant said **scornfully**.

Archie smiled. It was good to have a lighter moment during such an awful case as this. Chris North was quiet for a moment.

"Do you think this will work, sir?"

"The article? Let's hope so, Chris. We need all the help we can get."

Manchester United ist einer von 20 Fußballvereinen in der englischen **Premier League,** die seit 1992 die höchste Spielklasse in England ist. „ManU" ist mit 12 Meisterschaftstiteln englischer Rekordmeister.

Exercise 20: Questions about the text. **Beantworten Sie die Fragen zum Text!**

1. What have the police asked Rob to do?

   ____

2. Why did the police choose *Fans United*?

   ____

3. What football teams do DI McKay and Sergeant North support?

   ____

4. What did Greg Summers do for a living?

   ____

At the end of the day, Rob paused on the steps of the office to adjust his scarf and do up his coat. It had turned cold, dark and gloomy just in time for his journey home from the city centre. Rob waved as his colleague Michael whizzed past on his bike.

“See you tomorrow, Rob.”

“Home time!” said Rob to himself.

He couldn’t wait to get home, have a cold beer and tell Susan about his day. The visit from the police had been unsettling but exciting at the same time. The rest of the day had passed in a blur. He’d spent the afternoon writing the article and had emailed it to Sergeant North for approval.

to wave	winken
↯ to whizz past	vorbeirasen
unsettling	beunruhigend
to pass in a blur	wie im Flug vergehen

He'd had to stay late in order to finish his other work.
The rush hour was now over and the streets were deserted. It was only a short walk from the office to the bus stop, but it passed between now dark and empty office blocks. Rob dug in his pockets for his MP3 player. As he reached up to put the headphones in his ears, he had a strange feeling that he was being followed. He turned around. The wind had risen and was blowing litter across the pavements. There was no one there.
That's odd, thought Rob, feeling uneasy. He walked on but the feeling of being followed persisted.
A loud, unintelligible shout made him jump. He turned and saw a dark figure staggering up the road behind him. Rob began to walk faster.
The man shouted again, "Hey you!"

approval	Zustimmung, Freigabe
deserted	verlassen
to dig	*hier*: wühlen, suchen
litter	Müll
odd	seltsam, komisch
to persist	andauern, fortbestehen
unintelligible	unverständlich
to make sb. jump	jmd. zusammenzucken lassen

Exercise 21: Odd one out. Welches Wort ist das „schwarze Schaf"? Unterstreichen Sie!

1. strange normal odd unusual
2. dirty filthy clean greasy
3. exciting stimulating thrilling boring
4. deserted empty busy silent

filthy	dreckig
stubble	Bartstoppeln
threateningly	drohend
to edge backwards	sich langsam rückwärts bewegen
mute	stumm
to lurch	torkeln
↯ swig	Schluck
to hurl sth.	etw. schleudern

Rob glanced behind him and was shocked to recognize an all-too-familiar face. His heart thumped wildly in his chest. It was the man who had run into him the other night!
The serial killer, Rob thought, terrified. Oh my god!
The man was getting closer and closer. He was wearing the same filthy coat from before. His long dark hair was greasy and stubble covered his chin. He had a large, dirty rucksack on his back, and his hands were covered in tatty, dark woollen gloves.
"Oi, you!" he shouted threateningly.
Hurriedly, Rob walked on, almost running, as alarming thoughts rushed through his brain. Has he been waiting for me? How did he know where I work? Am I next?
Rob's legs turned to jelly and he felt as if he could hardly walk. He turned around to see where his pursuer was. To his horror, the man was only a few metres away.
"Are you all right there, mate?" he snarled.
"I…um…well…," stuttered Rob, edging backwards.
"Have you got a problem?"
He was so close now that Rob could see that the man's eyes were wild and unfocused. Rob shook his head. He was mute with terror.
Please let someone else come down the street, he thought desperately.
"Well, have you?" shouted the man with sudden explosive anger. He lurched towards Rob, reaching into the inner pocket of his dirty coat.

Oh god, he's got a knife! thought Rob. Adrenalin shot through his body. It was the kick he needed to get moving.
"Stay away!" screamed Rob. He was not going to let the killer get any closer to him.
The man staggered back a step. Rob turned and fled.
The aggressive-looking man was staring after him. He pulled a bottle out of his pocket and took a long swig. Then, with a furious roar, he hurled the bottle in Rob's direction. It smashed at Rob's feet as he raced off down the street. He didn't dare to look back.

Exercise 22: Translation quiz. Übersetzen Sie und enträtseln Sie das Lösungswort!

1. Bürgersteig _ _ _ _ □ _ _ _
2. Bartstoppeln _ _ □ _ _ _ _
3. vertraut _ _ _ _ _ _ _ □
4. zerzaust _ _ _ _ _ _ □
5. (Hosen-)Tasche _ _ _ _ □ _
6. Verfolger _ _ □ _ _ _ _
7. Kopfhörer _ □ _ _ _ _ _ _ _ _
8. Ärger _ _ _ _ □

Lösung: □□□□□□□□

The next evening, Susan and Rob went to one of their favourite Indian restaurants for dinner. They tried to do something roman-

demanding	anstrengend, anspruchsvoll
Managing Director	Geschäfts-führerin
bow	Verbeugung

tic with each other once a week – as if they were going on a date, even though they had now been together for several years. As it was a Tuesday and the restaurant was quiet, Rob and Susan were able to choose their seats. Susan selected a table in the front by the windows. While they waited for their food to arrive, they watched the people and cars passing by in the rain outside and talked about how their day had been.

"I've another big order coming in tomorrow," said Susan. "I'll need to go in early again."

She loved her job as a buyer for a big fashion company but it could be very demanding.

"The Managing Director will be coming in for the day. It's a good chance to impress her."

The couple held hands across the table. Rob looked at Susan and squeezed her hand. She looked up at him, her green eyes sparkling. She was wearing a flowing black top; her blonde hair was loose and fell around her face.

"I love you," he said.

She smiled. "I love you, too."

Just then, the waiter arrived at the table with their food. Slightly embarrassed, they let go of each other's hands. The waiter placed their dishes in front of them and left them with a polite bow. Rob took a mouthful of his curry. It was delicious.

Taking another bite, he glanced out of the window.

"I don't believe it!" he exclaimed.

"What?"

Rob pointed out of the window. "There, look! That's the man I was telling you about."

Exercise 23: Negatives. Verneinen Sie die folgenden Sätze!

1. Susan and Rob go out together once a week.

____

2. The restaurant was quiet.

____

3. They listened to the Indian music.

____

4. Susan and Rob are in love.

____

5. Susan is going to go into work early tomorrow.

____

Susan peered out of the window. "Who?"
"The guy who ran into me the day the body was found and who followed me yesterday!"
"Oh, the drunk you think is the serial killer!" Susan teased him. She leant across the table excitedly and scanned the street outside.
"Where, Rob? I can't see him."
"He's over there on the corner," Rob said.
The night before, when he came home and described his encounter to Susan, he'd clearly been quite shaken and she'd been

sympathetic	verständnisvoll
indulgent	nachsichtig, milde
to over-react	überreagieren
prospect	Aussicht
bemused	verwirrt, verständnislos
to leap to conclusions	voreilige Schlüsse ziehen
to illuminate	erleuchten
to rummage	kramen, wühlen
by chance	zufällig
to claim	behaupten
humiliating	demütigend
to shriek	kreischen

sympathetic – until he told her about the smashed bottle the man had thrown.
"He's obviously a drunk, Rob," she had said with an indulgent smile. "Don't you think you might have over-reacted a bit?"
Although he still felt a bit shaken, the prospect of getting the same bemused reaction from the police had stopped Rob from calling them. Maybe he had over-reacted.
After writing the article for the police all afternoon, the serial killer had been at the front of his mind. Maybe he'd leapt to conclusions. Now, looking at the man across the street, Rob wasn't so sure.
"Are you sure that's him?" asked Susan.
In the darkness and rain it was difficult to see clearly. The man was wearing a long dark coat and had a scarf wrapped over his head. Another car came along the road. Its headlights illuminated the man's face.
Rob was sure. "It's definitely him. Oh god, I think he's following me around!"
The man had been bent over and was rummaging in his rucksack. Now he straightened up and went to cross the road.
"What do you think, Susan? Should I report him to the police? He was in the area when the body was found. And he threw that bottle at me."

Exercise 24: Correct the mistakes. **Lesen Sie weiter und korrigieren Sie die sechs Fehler im folgenden Absatz!**

Susan shrugged. "I still thought it is very unlikely that the serial killer is an homeless man which you totally by chance ran into. But if you think it's important, then you should tell the police. Just remember that their really busy, and they probably get much calls from persons who claim to know who the killer is."

1. ____________________ 4. ____________________

2. ____________________ 5. ____________________

3. ____________________ 6. ____________________

"Yeah," said Rob thoughtfully. "I wouldn't want to waste their time." He really did not want to have to tell the police about the bottle incident. It had been a scary and humiliating experience.

"It's probably nothing anyway," he added.

A thumping on the window made them both jump. Susan shrieked. The homeless man was banging on the window right by their table and was shouting drunkenly. It was impossible to understand what he was saying. The man's eyes were mad and angry as he gestured at them and banged the window again. The waiters raced to the door and shouted at the man to move on. With one last bang on the window, he staggered off.

Rob looked at Susan. Her face was white, her eyes wide open.

"Rob, you need to call the police."

4 A SMALL WORLD

The killer sat alone in the dark. The curtains were still open and the light from the streetlights outside created strange shadows across the room. He sank down lower in his armchair. His thoughts were racing and his foot was tapping a nervous rhythm on the floor. He felt so much freer here. He'd not had a safe, proper home for so long. It was only here, in his own space, that he didn't have to hide anything. He could completely be himself.

to tap	(leicht) klopfen
outline	Umriss
to erase	auslöschen, ausradieren
to taunt	verspotten, herausfordern
hatred	Hass
to boil	kochen
to tense	(sich) anspannen
pile	Stapel
smart	*hier*: schick

Through the darkness he could see the outline of the seven photographs on the wall. He couldn't see the faces in the photographs, but he didn't need to. By now they were as familiar to him as his own face. He could picture them in his mind every time he closed his eyes. He knew every detail, even of those with the faces crossed out. Angry, black pen marks had erased the faces of his victims, just as he had removed them from their families, their lives and their friends. But the remaining faces taunted him. Their happiness, comfort and security contrasted so strongly with his own life. Smiling from the end of the row was Rob's face.

He felt the hatred boiling inside him. He could almost taste it – a bitter, sour taste at the back of his throat. Every muscle in his body tensed as he sat in his chair, clenching his fists. Breathing slowly, he forced himself to relax. He knew he needed to be careful and clever. He mustn't get caught. He couldn't be. They had taken so much from him already.

Exercise 25: Adjectives. Ergänzen Sie die fehlenden Steigerungsformen!

1. strange	___________	___________
2. ___________	angrier	___________
3. ___________	___________	lowest
4. happy	___________	___________
5. comfortable	___________	___________

"Susan, just sit down! You're making me nervous!" Rob said.
Susan adjusted the cushions on the sofa one last time before sitting down.
"I don't know what's wrong with me," she said as she straightened a pile of papers on the coffee table.
"The police are just coming to hear what we have to say. It's not as if they've heard about the pile of stolen banknotes in your wardrobe," joked Rob.
"Oh, ha ha," replied Susan sarcastically, but she visibly relaxed. Rob noticed she had put on a smart blue shirt and black skirt for the police visit, even though it was her Friday off. Rob was wearing his usual jeans, shirt and jumper. For a second he wondered

if he ought to have worn a tie, before telling himself he was being ridiculous. Rob was going into work later. Being a journalist gave him some flexibility with his hours.
"I've never really spoken to the police before," Susan added.
"Me neither," said Rob.
Despite his jokes, he was also feeling tense. Reporting their encounters with that dirty, aggressive man had seemed like the right thing to do, but now he had his doubts. What if they were wasting police time while the serial killer was still out there?
The bell to the flat rang. Susan leapt up from her seat. She smoothed her clothes and tucked her hair behind her ears.
"Hello again," said Detective Inspector McKay as he entered the living room.
"Hello, Inspector," said Rob, shaking his hand and nodding at Sergeant North.

Exercise 26: Prepositions. Lesen Sie weiter und setzen Sie die Präpositionen richtig ein!

opposite | out | into | at | on

The policemen sat down **1.** ______ the sofa. Sergeant North took **2.** ______ his notebook. Susan went **3.** ______ the kitchen to make cups of tea, while Rob took a seat **4.** ______ the policemen. He **fiddled** nervously with his fingers. Detective Inspector McKay smiled **5.** ______ him **encouragingly**.

Uncountable Nouns
Unzählbare Nomen wie **information, news, advice, furniture, money, water** usw. haben keine Pluralform und ihnen folgt das Verb in der Einzahl: *There is no information on this topic. The news was really shocking.* Um eine genaue Menge anzugeben, ergänzt man die **uncountable nouns** mit einer Mengenangabe:
a piece of information
some good news
a glass of water

"Thank you for calling us," he said. "Any information[i] is really appreciated. Thank you for the article as well. It was exactly what we were looking for."
Rob nodded. "You're very welcome."
DI McKay continued, "You said on the phone that you may have some information for us. Please tell us what happened."
Rob explained his collision with the man on the night Greg Summers' body had been found. Susan came to sit next to him and put her hand on his knee as he spoke. DI McKay asked the occasional question.
"So this man had blood on his coat?"
"Yes," confirmed Rob. "He was holding his hand against his chest and it looked as if he had blood down the front of his coat."
Sergeant North scribbled notes in his book as Rob talked. He looked up in interest as Rob described the encounter in the street with the smashed bottle and the scene at the restaurant. Finally DI McKay stood up.
"I know it sounds a bit far-fetched and silly," said Rob slightly embarrassed, "but I had wondered if this man is following me."
"It doesn't sound silly at all," said Archie. "Thank you again,

to fiddle	herumspielen
encouragingly	aufmunternd
to appreciate sth.	etw. zu schätzen wissen
to scribble	(hin)kritzeln
far-fetched	weit hergeholt

to follow up on sth.	etw. weiterverfolgen, einer Sache nachgehen
feature	großer Artikel
to label	beschriften, betiteln
⚡ pest	⚡ Nervensäge, Plage
wryly	trocken, ironisch

Rob. We will definitely follow up on this information."

As Sergeant North stood, he caught sight of the top sheet on the pile of paper on the coffee table. The red and white team colours on the photograph caught his eye.

"What's this?" he asked, lifting it up for a proper look.

"Oh, that's an article I wrote," explained Rob. "It was for the fifteenth anniversary of the Manchester United Coach Massacre. The magazine ran a big feature on it."

Sergeant North studied the article with interest.

"I was supposed to be at the match that day but was sick, so I had to stay at home," said Rob.

"This is your father?" asked Sergeant North shocked, pointing at one of the article's photographs.

"No," said Rob taking the article from him. "It's a photograph of one of the victims. He worked with my dad and had used the tickets when we couldn't go. There was a mistake during editing the article and the picture was labelled wrongly. My dad is still alive and still a pest."

He smiled wryly.

Detective Inspector McKay broke the silence. "Well, thank you again, Rob. It was nice to meet you, Susan."

Rob and Susan rose and escorted the two policemen to the door of the flat. DI McKay turned to them.

"We'll let you know if anything comes from our enquiries," he added. "And if you see the man again, call the police immediately. We want to speak to him."

Exercise 27: Crossword puzzle. Lösen Sie das Kreuzworträtsel!

Across

1. a picture made with a camera

5. Sergeant North is a police ...

7. the police asked Rob to write one of these.

Down

2. red liquid inside your body

3. *Fans United* is a ...

4. a warm item of outdoor clothing

6. the opposite of "to tense"

patrol car	Streifenwagen
incident room	Einsatzzentrale
to circulate sth.	etw. herumgeben, in Umlauf bringen
roundabout	Kreisverkehr
flurry of activity	Hektik
Well, well!	Na, sowas! Na, sieh mal einer an!
tree-lined	von Bäumen gesäumt
detached house	freistehendes Haus
to mow	mähen

"What do you make of that, sir?" asked Sergeant North as they climbed back into the police car.

"Well, it's certainly worth pursuing," said DI McKay. "This man was acting very suspiciously in the area of a crime. We need to find him. Call the station with his description, Chris. I want every patrol car looking out for him."

Sergeant North took out his mobile phone and called the incident room. "Hello Teresa, can you circulate a description of a suspect for me, please..."

Detective Inspector McKay turned the car onto the main road. His mind was turning over the discussion with Rob. Had they finally got their lead? Had someone actually seen the killer? It was a small chance, but they needed everything they could get at the moment.

He slowed as they approached a roundabout. (i) The next person on their list didn't live too far away. Now that the initial flurry of activity following the discovery of a body was over, the investigators were back to following up all leads. This meant talking to many people, asking a lot of questions and trying to work out if the huge amount of information they gath-

Achtung Linksverkehr!
Jeder weiß, dass in Großbritannien, Irland und den meisten Staaten des Commonwealth Linksverkehr herrscht. Daneben sind auch Kreisverkehre viel häufiger als in Deutschland (es gibt sie selbst auf Autobahnen!) und es gibt keine automatische Rechts-vor-links-Regel. Die Vorfahrt wird immer durch Verkehrszeichen angegeben.

ered contained anything useful. It was hard work and they had to concentrate. They couldn't afford to miss that one little detail which may one day lead to their killer.

"…Thanks, Teresa. See you later," said Chris as he switched off his phone.

He turned to his boss. "Well, well! It's a small world, sir. Greg Summers did spend time in prison. Guess what for?"

The Detective Inspector looked at his sergeant with interest. "Go on…"

"Thirteen years ago, Greg Summers served three years in prison. He sold the guns that were used in the Manchester United coach massacre!"

Exercise 28: Fill in the blanks. Lesen Sie weiter und ergänzen Sie die fehlenden Wörter!

garage boot driveway lock lawn noon

Just before 1. ______ on Saturday, Max drove up the tree-lined 2. ______ towards his luxurious, detached house. He parked the BMW in front of the double 3. ______, collected his golf shoes from the car 4. ______ and made his way to the large front door. As he put the key in the 5. ______, he noticed one of the gardeners mowing the wide front 6. ______.

to curse	fluchen
to put up with sth.	etw. aushalten, etw. ertragen
to discard	ablegen, fallen lassen
patio	Terrasse
Great Dane	Deutsche Dogge
stable	Stall
irritating	ärgerlich
hum	Brummen, Knattern
to pour sth.	etw. einschenken

Max nodded at him and said, "Good morning."

The man nodded back. His baseball cap was pulled down low, hiding his face. Max cursed as he entered the house. His wife Cynthia had hired the gardening company. He couldn't deny that they did a great job, but you just never knew when they were going to arrive. With Cynthia and his daughters out at horse riding lessons, he had been looking forward to having the house to himself for a few hours. Now there was this gardener and the noise of his lawnmower to put up with.

Exercise 29: Word order. Bringen Sie die Wörter in die richtige Reihenfolge!

1. cursed entered Max as house the he

____

2. sign dogs there no the was of

____

3. It day a autumn warm relatively was

____

4. doors patio the he glass opened

____

Muttering to himself, Max dumped his golf shoes on the floor at the bottom of the stairs. Cynthia would have something to say about the clumps of grass on the cream carpet, but he wasn't too worried. The cleaner was coming tomorrow and she might as well have something to clean, thought Max as he discarded his jacket on the chair in the hall.

Cricket ist im ganzen britischen Commonwealth ein sehr beliebter Mannschaftssport, der auf einem ovalen Spielfeld gespielt wird. Jede Mannschaft zählt 11 Spieler, die alle in weiß gekleidet sind. Ein Cricketspiel dauert für gewöhnlich 5 Tage, wobei pro Tag 3 mal 2 Stunden gespielt wird. So werden die Spieler bezeichnet:

bowler	Werfer
batsman	Schlagmann
fielder	Fänger/Feldspieler

"Baxter! Wilf!" He whistled, but there was no sign of the dogs. "Come here, boys!"

Max wandered into the large, comfortable living room to the back of the house. He opened the glass patio doors and called again.

"Wilf! Baxter!"

He let out a long whistle, but there was no sign of the two Great Danes. Odd, he thought. Cynthia must have taken them to the stables with her.

It was a relatively warm autumn day and a pleasant breeze was blowing. The irritating hum of the lawnmower was even louder with the door open, but the fresh air was nice. He went to the drinks cabinet and poured himself a small brandy.

Max took his drink into the study, settled himself in his large, brown leather armchair in the centre of the room and turned on the television. The sun was shining on the cricket pitch [i] in Melbourne as the English bowler threw the ball at the Australian batsman. He was caught out by England's star fielder.

"Well done, chaps!" Max said out loud.

to retrieve	zurückholen
to snap	blaffen
sb.'s heart sinks	jmd. rutscht das Herz in die Hose
↯ scum	Abschaum
thug	Schlägertyp
to get the better of sb.	über jmd. die Oberhand gewinnen
to be in charge of sth.	befehlen, am Drücker sitzen
to betray sb.	jmd. verraten
to flicker	flackern
conscious	bei Bewusstsein

He leaned forward eagerly in his chair, his glass held loosely between his fingers. The sound of the lawnmower seemed to have stopped, thank God, and so the TV commentary was clearer now. As the next Australian batsman made his way towards the centre of the pitch, Max heard a slight sound from the living room. He turned his head a little without taking his eyes off the screen. He saw the new batsman swing his bat and the red ball fly towards the pitch boundary. The sound from the living room was forgotten as the fielders ran to **retrieve** the ball.

"Come on, come on!"

Suddenly he became aware of a presence behind him. He tried to turn but at the same instant, the cold, hard edge of a blade was pressed against his neck. He dropped his glass in shock.

"Don't move a muscle," a low male voice spoke in his ear.

Max froze. Looking up out of corner of his eye, he could see the edge of his attacker's baseball cap. It was the gardener. He was sure of it.

"What is the meaning of this?" **snapped** Max. "If it's money you want then take it. There is cash in the safe behind the desk."

"Typical," came the angry voice from behind him. "It's not always about money, you know."

Max's **heart sank**. From his years working on criminal cases he knew that personal crimes were more likely to become violent.

That wouldn't happen to him though, he was sure. Max had met this sort of scum before, and he wouldn't let this thug get the better of him. He wouldn't let his attacker see he was scared. "Well, what is it you want from me then?" retorted Max, confident he could still get rid of his attacker.
He was used to being in charge and couldn't fully comprehend the seriousness of the situation he was in.
"I want you to realize what you have done and then I want you to suffer," said the man.
Max gasped in fear. "What? I don't even know who you are!"

Exercise 30: Adjective or adverb? Lesen Sie weiter und ergänzen Sie die richtige Form!

"No one ever does," replied the gardener 1. bitter ________________.

With an 2. ugly ____________ snarl, he drew the blade 3. sharp ____________________ across Max's throat.

"But I'll tell you what you did...," he whispered 4. cold ________________ in his victim's ear. "You betrayed us."

Max's eyes widened in horror as his blood sprayed across the room. The killer laughed manically as the red splashes hit the walls.
The killer walked round to stand in front of the chair as his victim's head sank down on his chest. Max's eyelids flickered desperately as he struggled to remain conscious. The killer's hate-filled eyes were the last thing he saw. Max let out a final, hideous

gaping	klaffend
trickle	Tropfen, Rinnsal
corpse	Leiche
to sleep soundly	tief und fest schlafen
kennel	Zwinger
anxiously	besorgt
instrumental	entscheidend

gurgle. The blood, which had been pumping furiously from the gaping wound, now slowed to a trickle. The killer grabbed Max by the hair and pulled his head up. His eyes were dead and empty.

"No!" whispered the killer. "NO!"

This death had been too easy. The killer couldn't risk a repeat of the struggle and noise from last time but now he felt robbed. Max should have suffered like he had done. The man who had betrayed him so hugely had slipped away from life in a matter of seconds. The anger exploded inside him.

Exercise 31: Match-up. Welche der folgenden Synonyme gehören zusammen? Ordnen Sie zu!

1. ☐ comprehend	a) struggle
2. ☐ fight	b) final
3. ☐ retrieve	c) understand
4. ☐ violent	d) get back
5. ☐ last	e) aggressive

"NO!" he shouted.

He brought the knife down again and again. The knife ripped holes in Max's now bright-red golf jumper and sliced into his flesh. He stabbed and kicked the body in fury, but Max had escaped again.

Finally his anger died away and the killer realized what he was doing. He took a deep breath and fought to get himself under control. Max's bloodied body lay on the floor at the foot of his chair. Betrayer, thought the killer. He took one more slow, deep breath and smiled. I am back in charge. Untouchable! he thought.
The killer wiped his bloodied knife on the arm of the chair. He took one last look at the corpse before slipping silently out of the building through the patio doors. The drugged dogs still slept soundly in their large wooden kennel at the side of the house.

Susan and Rob were shopping in Manchester city centre. Susan's theory that 'it would be much quieter on a Sunday' had proved incorrect. As they pushed through the crowds in the Arndale Centre, Rob thought how much he would rather be almost anywhere else.
"I'll just be a couple of minutes, I promise."
Rob sighed as Susan disappeared into yet another changing room with yet another armful of dresses. Bored, he wandered towards the front of the shop.
Suddenly, his mobile phone rang. "Hello?"
"Good afternoon, Mr Anderson. This is Sergeant Teresa Marsh from Didsbury Police Station. I understand you recently spoke to my colleagues Detective Inspector McKay and Sergeant North?"
"Yes, I did. Is there a problem?" asked Rob anxiously.
"No, not at all," replied Sergeant Marsh warmly. "We have followed up on your information, and the Detective Inspector has asked me to pass on what we found out."
Rob tensed as the blood roared in his ears. Was he going to hear that they had solved the case? Had he been instrumental in the hunt for a serial killer?

CCTV footage	Überwachungs-video(s)
backyard	Hinterhof
trespassing	unbefugtes Betreten
cheerfully	gut gelaunt, fröhlich

Sergeant Marsh continued, "We have identified the man from CCTV footage from near the scene where you ran into him, and we spoke to him this morning…"

Rob held his breath.

"The gentleman in question is well known to the local police. He is homeless and has a problem with alcohol. Officers have spoken to him several times. On each occasion members of the public had called saying he was drunk and being aggressive."

"I see," said Rob. He realized this wasn't going to be the breakthrough he'd imagined.

"…on the night of Mr Summers' murder, this homeless gentleman was sleeping in the backyard of a nearby restaurant. He was woken up by the sound of our police sirens and panicked. He thought someone had reported him for trespassing. In his hurry to leave the yard, he slipped and cut his hand on some broken glass. We've tested it and the only blood on his coat was his."

"Oh, okay," said Rob, feeling stupid for wasting their time.

"Thank you for calling us," replied Sergeant Marsh cheerfully as she ended the call. "It is very much appreciated. We're dependent on members of the public to report suspicious behaviour; it's how we're going to catch this killer."

5 A LEAD?

heated argument	hitziger/heftiger Streit
accusingly	vorwurfsvoll

Tuesday had started as a good day but it was not ending well. Rob and Susan had been talking about their weekend plans over dinner. Somehow their conversation had turned into a heated argument.

"You promised you would come to my mother's house this Saturday!" Susan said, accusingly.

"I don't remember saying that at all," Rob snapped back. "Anyway, why would I agree to visit your mother when I know I have to work?"

Exercise 32: Verb forms? Lesen Sie weiter und ergänzen Sie die passende Verbform!

get   watch   make   stand   reply

"I don't think **1.** ______ a football match classes as work."

"That's a bit harsh, Susan," he **2.** ______. "You know what my job involves."

"But you promised, Rob!"

Susan **3.** ______ up and began to gather the dinner plates together noisily. She marched into the kitchen and turned on both the radio and the taps. Rob sighed before **4.** ______ up to join her in the kitchen.

"I'm sorry," he said trying to **5.** ______ it up to her.

Susan didn't turn around. She was furiously clattering the pots and pans around in the sink.

"I really am sorry," he said to her back. "If I could get out of going to the match, I would."

"Hrmph."

"I would."

"Whatever, Rob. My mum has specially bought a leg of lamb to roast and Auntie Elsa is coming to visit as well."

Rob rolled his eyes behind her back. Even if he had been able to go, the prospect of an afternoon with miserable, complaining Auntie Elsa was not appealing! At that moment the voice on the radio caught his attention.

"...Who?"

"And another thing...," Susan continued indignantly.

"Wait, stop talking," said Rob without thinking.

She turned towards him with a face like thunder. "Don't tell me to stop talking!"

He took her gently by the shoulders. "Susan, just be quiet for one minute, please!"

She looked hurt but stopped talking. Rob turned the volume up on the radio.

"...The murder of Judge Maximillian Fitzwilliam-Herbert-Smythe three days ago has now been officially linked to the serial killer investigation."

"I don't believe it!" Rob gasped. "I've heard that name before."

Susan looked confused. "What? Who? How?"

"Maximillian Fitzwilliam-Herbert-Smythe!" he said earnestly, walking out of the kitchen. "He appeared in the last edition of *Fans United*. I'm sure of it."

Rob rummaged around in his rucksack in the hall to find the latest edition of the magazine. Leafing through the pages, he found the article he was looking for. He then raced to his laptop in the living room. He had been working on an article before his argument with Susan. Taking a seat on the sofa, he lifted the computer onto his lap. The screensaver disappeared as he touched the keyboard.

to clatter	klappern, poltern
miserable	unglücklich, griesgrämig
indignantly	entrüstet, aufgebracht
face like thunder	finstere Miene
earnestly	ernst(haft)
to leaf through sth.	etw. durchblättern
robe	Richterrobe

Susan followed him into the living room, their argument forgotten.

"Look at this," he said, showing her the screen and the article. "I knew I was right."

He had entered a search for the judge's name and the word murder. The first site that came up was a recent BBC news article:

Top Judge Murdered - City in Fear!

A photograph of the judge in his robe was displayed above the text. There was no doubt: the murdered judge and the 'fan of the week' were the same man.

Exercise 33: Conjunctions. Verbinden Sie die Sätze mit der richtigen Konjunktion!

and when as but

1. "Why would I agree to visit your mother? I know I have to work."

2. The screensaver disappeared. He touched the keyboard.

3. "My mum has specially bought a leg of lamb to roast. Auntie Elsa is coming to visit as well."

4. She looked hurt. She stopped talking.

coincidence	Zufall
maniac	Wahnsinniger, Irrer

Rob felt a cold sweat break out on the back of his neck. He looked up at Susan's shocked face.
"What is going on?" he asked. "It must be a coincidence."
"Surely the killer wouldn't have chosen his victim from a photograph in a magazine?" said Susan.
Rob let the magazine fall to the ground. The serial killer had been terrorising the city for weeks. The story had been dominating the newspaper and television reports. The people of Manchester were nervous. They knew they weren't safe in their own homes. Rob's head was thumping. He was a normal man; he led a normal life and yet he had had two links with the serial killer in less than a week. A murder victim had been found not far from the flat he shared with Susan, and then a man who had featured in the magazine he worked for had been killed in a brutal fashion. And then there were his discussions with the police and the collision with the homeless man. He shuddered.
He took Susan's hand and stared earnestly into her eyes. "Promise me you'll be careful until this maniac is caught."

Exercise 34: Translation. Übersetzen Sie folgende Sätze!

1. "What is going on?" he asked. "It must be a coincidence."

____

2. Rob let the magazine fall to the ground.

____

3. A murder victim had been found not far from his flat.

____

4. "Promise me you'll be careful."

____

The next morning Rob entered the offices of *Fans United* and marched straight over to James's desk. He dropped the previous day's edition of the *Manchester Evening News* down on James's keyboard. The face of the murdered judge stared out from below the headline **Serial killer strikes top judge.**

"What do you make of this?" he demanded.

James looked up at him, confused. "What on earth do you mean?"

"This was your latest 'fan of the week'! He has been murdered."

"Pardon?"

"Murdered, James! He was killed by the serial killer. You featured him in your column last week and now he's dead."

James picked up the newspaper. He didn't like what he thought Rob was implying.

"Just what are you saying, Rob?" he replied angrily. "It must be a coincidence. This man may not even have been 'fan of the week'."

"Oh, he is," Rob replied. "I checked. Don't you recognize his face? And then there is that name. It's so distinctive."

James tossed the newspaper aside. He typed the judge's name into his internet search engine.

"Look, I bet there are several Maximillian Fitzwilliam-Herbert… whatevers."

Rob snorted. "I doubt there is more than one set of parents who would be that cruel!"

He felt strangely out of control. The feeling had stayed with him since he had heard the news of the judge's death the night before. After the disturbing events of the past few days, it felt good to vent some of his tension, even if it was on James.

headline	Schlagzeile
to imply sth.	etw. andeuten
distinctive	unverwechselbar
to toss sth.	werfen, schleudern
disturbing	verstörend, beunruhigend
to vent	ablassen, (sich) Luft machen
to concede	eingestehen, zugeben
to be beyond reproach	über jeden Tadel erhaben sein
verdict	Urteil

"Well?" he snapped.

James was silent for a few seconds as he read the results on the screen.

"...it seems you are right," he finally conceded. "Judge Maximillian Fitzwilliam-Herbert-Smythe was murdered on Saturday."

He read on. "Hey, look at this!"

James turned the computer screen around. "Our judge has been all over the news in the past few months. He was the judge who released Jared Cook, the gunman from the 1996 coach massacre."

"No way!" said Rob, reading the first article.

"...Judge Fitzwilliam-Herbert-Smythe stated after the success of Mr Cook's appeal, 'It is essential that the integrity of the legal process is maintained. Questions remain over the original investigation. Our police must be beyond reproach. Therefore I am freeing Mr Cook. I apologize to the families of the victims as I understand today's verdict raises more questions for them. However, criminal trials must be fair and honest. Justice must be seen to be done.'"

"This wasn't justice," Rob **fumed**. "'Mr' Cook should have stayed locked up and they should have thrown away the key!"

Exercise 35: Who said what? Wer sagte was? Kreuzen Sie an!

1. "Justice must be seen to be done."
   a) ❒ Jared Cook
   b) ❒ Rob
   c) ❒ Judge Fitzwilliam-Herbert-Smythe

2. "Don't you recognize his face?"
   a) ❒ Rob
   b) ❒ James
   c) ❒ George Jenkins

3. "What on earth do you mean?"
   a) ❒ James
   b) ❒ Detective Inspector McKay
   c) ❒ Sergeant North

4. "The man deserves better. They all do."
   a) ❒ Rob
   b) ❒ Detective Inspector McKay
   c) ❒ Judge Fitzwilliam-Herbert-Smythe

to fume	vor Wut schäumen
temple	*hier*: Schläfe
unbearable	unerträglich
witness statement	Zeugenaussage
to retire	in Rente gehen
plumber	Klemptner

Detective Inspector McKay laid his head in his hands and rubbed his **temples**. He was exhausted. The murder of Judge Fitzwilliam-Herbert-Smythe three days ago had increased the pressure on the investigative team even more. The attention on DI McKay and his colleagues had become almost **unbearable**.

Archie sighed. "What are we missing, Chris? The answers must be here somewhere."

He gestured at the chaotic incident room. Sheets of information, photographs and **witness statements** were everywhere.

"Let's start again. What do we know about the victims?" Sergeant North began. "Our first victim was George Jenkins. He was fifty-six and a lorry driver whose job took him all over the country. The second victim was Tony Carmichael. He spent twenty years as a policeman on this force before he **retired** and we still can't find his killer."

"The man deserves better. They all do," said Archie.

Chris continued with his description. "Our third victim was Josh Cameron, thirty-five, a **plumber**. All the victims lived in the Greater Manchester area. They didn't know each other; they didn't go to the same places. We haven't been able to find a single link between them."

DI McKay nodded. "All our victims have been male but there is no other pattern. They are different ages. They look completely different. They live miles apart from each other. The only similarity is the killer's method. Each body was found with multiple stab wounds."

Exercise 36: Fill in the blanks. Lesen Sie weiter und setzen Sie die Begriffe richtig ein!

motive · files · notebook · prison · taxi

Sergeant North **consulted** his **1.** ______ again. "Greg Summers, the fourth victim, was a **2.** ______ driver. He spent time in **3.** ______ for selling the gun that was used in the Manchester United coach massacre. We've looked through all his **4.** ______ to find a possible **5.** ______ for our serial killer, sir. But nothing **leaps out**. Although..."

"What is it, Chris?"

"I did a background check on all our victims and Tony Carmichael's name appeared in a news article several years ago."

DI McKay looked at him with interest.

"It was never proved and the officer's name has never been released, but this article speculated that Tony Carmichael was responsible for the **tainted evidence** that eventually freed Jared Cook, the gunman at the coach massacre."

"And our most recent victim also had links to the massacre! It was Judge Fitzwilliam-Herbert-Smythe who released Mr Cook from prison. This could be it, Chris," he said excitedly, "...the break we've been waiting for!"

"The coach massacre, sir?" Chris said sceptically.

"Yes."

"There's a tentative link between three of our victims and the shooting, but how do the other victims fit?"
"I don't know, Chris, but it's the first link we've found in the whole of this horrendous case. Maybe it's just a coincidence, but we need to be sure."
"It can't be Jared Cook," said Sergeant North. "You know that the cold case squad have been monitoring him since his release. They want to see if the second gunman gets in touch after all this time."
"Aye," DI McKay replied, "but what about Michael Sullivan's relatives and business 'acquaintances'. The shooting of such a high-profile gangster and his killer's release is going to stir up strong emotions and feelings of revenge in the criminal underworld."
"Yes," added Sergeant North excitedly. "And then there are the victims' relatives. They aren't going to be happy. You can't deny that the serial killings have all started since Jared Cook was released."
DI McKay pursed his lips thoughtfully. "We need to be cautious here. It's a definite lead, but it could still be a coincidence. We'll continue working on all our other lines of enquiry, but I want some men on this. We need a list of everyone even remotely connected with the coach massacre. Chris, I want you to start working on this. Get Sergeant Marsh to help you."
Sergeant North jumped up from his seat enthusiastically. "I'll go and find Teresa now."

to consult sth.	*hier*: nachsehen/nachschlagen in
ϟ to leap out	*hier*: hervorstechen, auffallen
tainted evidence	fingierte/nicht verwertbare Beweise
tentative	vorläufig, provisorisch
cold case squad	Dezernat für ungeklärte Fälle
acquaintance	Bekannter
to stir up	entfachen, aufwirbeln
to purse one's lips	den Mund verziehen
line of enquiry	Untersuchungsrichtung
remotely	entfernt

Exercise 37: Pronouns. **Ersetzen Sie die markierten Wörter durch die entsprechenden Pronomen und schreiben Sie die Sätze neu!**

1. **Detective Inspector McKay** laid his head in his hands.

   ____

2. **The victims** lived in the Greater Manchester area.

   ____

3. "It can't be **Jared Cook**," said Sergeant North.

   ____

4. "I'll go and find **Teresa** now."

   ____

The low hum of conversation filled the room as the rich and famous mingled with the members of the press. The hospitality suite at Old Trafford was full on this Thursday night.

"Good evening, Rob."

The Club Chairman nodded at Rob as he walked past, a much younger, famous soap star on his arm.

"Good evening," replied Rob. After a moment, he started grinning: Celebrity was obvi-

to mingle	sich mischen
hospitality suite	Besucherlounge, VIP-Lounge
to be signed	unter Vertrag genommen werden
posh	vornehm, piekfein
well-groomed	gepflegt
stooped	altersgebeugt
embroidered	gestickt

ously attractive. Rob grabbed a glass of champagne from a tray carried by a bored-looking waiter and went to stand in a quiet corner. As one of the main reporters of such a recognized fan magazine, Rob had been invited to many of these events in the past. He was always interested in meeting the new stars, but essentially these events were all the same. Every time a new football star was signed, the press were invited to a posh reception to meet him. The same drinks were served; the same comments were made by the manager and the well-groomed new recruit. Rob yawned.

Exercise 38: Missing verbs. Lesen Sie weiter und bringen Sie die Verben in die richtige Form!

"Are we **1.** keep ________ you from your bed?" joked a voice from behind him.

Rob **2.** turn ________ around. A stooped man with white hair and a mischievous grin **3.** stand ________ behind him. He **4.** wear ________ a smart dark-blue uniform with 'caretaker' embroidered on the chest pocket.

Rob **5.** smile ________. "Sorry, it's been a busy few days."

The man extended his hand, which Rob **6.** shake ________.

fuss	Getue, Wirbel
to survey	überblicken
ϟ snap	Schnappschuss
notable	berühmt, bekannt
ϟ bigwig	ϟ hohes Tier

"It's always the same, eh?" the caretaker commented, gesturing with his head at the party going on around them. "Look at all this fuss and money for some new young chap who won't be here five minutes," he continued in a bemused voice. "I've been here 25 years and I sometimes think no one notices me unless the bins aren't emptied."

"Ha ha," laughed Rob. "You could try scoring a couple of goals in a major competition match. Then you'd get more champagne than you could ever wish for!"

The caretaker laughed heartily. "I'll bear that in mind. See you later, mate."

"Bye for now."

Rob leaned back against the wall as his eyes surveyed the room. He was pleased to see Will making his way through the crowd towards him.

"Hi, Will. What are you doing here?" Rob asked in surprise.

Will grinned. "I'm a bit of a photographer in my spare time. I'd like to develop it into a career if I can. I showed the editor some of my snaps and asked if I could get some work experience." He gestured at the room. "And here I am!"

"Good for you," Rob said warmly. He really liked Will and began to point out notable people. "Kevin will be expecting photos of them."

"Excellent! Thanks, Rob," Will said, lifting his camera to his eye. "I've never been this close to all the bigwigs!"

"Don't worry, it took me a while to get used to it as well. I used to come to every match with my dad – but this is something else! Did you come much as a child?"

"Occasionally," Will replied in a low voice without moving his face from the camera's viewfinder.

Exercise 39: Hidden words. **Finden Sie die zehn gesuchten Wörter!**

C	A	R	E	T	A	K	E	R	A
O	Q	R	T	A	Y	I	N	A	T
M	B	A	K	X	S	F	T	U	C
P	E	Y	P	I	L	O	R	H	A
E	Q	Z	O	L	O	C	A	L	M
T	D	C	R	O	W	D	N	I	E
I	U	I	T	K	A	N	C	V	R
T	W	J	U	D	G	E	E	S	A
I	I	D	G	L	B	E	A	X	R
O	P	Z	A	J	M	D	P	W	O
N	R	E	L	A	T	I	V	E	S

1. an event which people want to win by being the best
2. members of a family
3. Greg Summers drove a ...
4. the country immediately west of Spain
5. close to or belonging to the area
6. a person who looks after a building
7. the opposite of exit
8. This person can send you to prison or set you free.
9. a large group of people
10. You take photographs with this.

commotion	Tumult, Unruhe
to glint	glitzern
shaft	Strahl
razor-sharp	rasiermesserscharf
rootless	heimatlos, entwurzelt
unsuspecting	ahnungslos, nichts ahnend
savage	brutal, wild

A commotion by the entrance prevented any further conversation. Enrique Garamay, the team's latest signing from Portugal, had arrived. His supermodel girlfriend was sticking close to his side as the gathered members of the press went wild.
"...Enrique! Enrique!"

A few hours later, the killer smiled lovingly at the blade as it glinted in the shaft of moonlight coming through a crack in the curtains. Carefully, he ran a cloth along the razor-sharp edge. There was no trace left of the knife's recent brutal activities. The killer grasped the heavy handle tightly. With the knife in his hand he felt powerful. The anxious, rootless feeling of the past few years was gone. Now he felt like the master of his universe.
He rose from his chair, switched on the lamp and strode across the room. With his knife held tightly in his right hand, he looked at the line of photographs on the wall. The judge's face was now crossed out. Thick black lines slashed across his face, much like the pattern the knife had left on the judge's body. In many ways the judge had started this chain of bloody events and now he was gone. The killer smiled. He turned his attention to the next photograph and used the edge of his blade to scratch a circle around the smiling face.
"I hope you are ready," he said to the unsuspecting face. "You're next. I am coming for you."
The thought of his next victim made his hands tremble in excitement. His revenge was going to be sweet and savage.

6 JUST A COINCIDENCE

to wag	wedeln
yelp	Kleffen, Gebell
worktop	Arbeitsfläche

Judith bent over to fill Katie's bowl with dog biscuits. The little white terrier's tail **wagged** furiously as she buried her face in the dish. Judith ran her hands over the little dog's back and was rewarded with a contented **yelp**.

"Aww, good girl, Katie."

Exercise 40: Simple past or past perfect? Lesen Sie weiter und setzen Sie die richtige Verbform ein!

Judith **1.** collect ______________ her cup of tea from the **worktop** and **2.** put ______________ another couple of biscuits on the saucer. I'll burn them off later when I take Katie for a walk, she lied to herself. She **3.** put on ______________ several pounds since she **4.** finish ______________ working. She missed being a nurse, but it **5.** not take ______________ her long to get used to lazier days **6.** fill ______________ with soap operas and chatting with her friends.

to pad	tappen, trotten
terraced house	Reihenhaus
tucked	geklemmt, gesteckt
↯ to have a natter	↯ quatschen
to growl	knurren
goosebumps *pl*	Gänsehaut
to thrust	stoßen

The doorbell interrupted her thoughts. She padded down the hall of her small terraced house in her purple, fluffy slippers, her tea in one hand and a magazine tucked under her arm.

This must be Ivy, she thought to herself. It was almost time for Monday night's episode of *Coronation Street*[i] to start. Since they'd both retired, they had got into the habit of watching the soap opera together a couple of evenings a week. It was nice to have company because her husband had died, and it was good to have a natter.

Beaming, she turned the key and swung the door open wide.

"Hi love!...Oh…sorry. I thought you were someone else."

As soon as she saw the stranger at the door, Judith felt uneasy. The man was wearing a smooth, black raincoat and his baseball cap was pulled down low over his face.

"Can I help you?" she asked nervously.

"Remember me?" the stranger growled.

Judith was sure she had never seen him before. And there was something about his appearance and the way he spoke that gave her goosebumps. Instinctively, she tried to push the door closed, but the man was too quick for her and thrust it open again. Judith was pushed back violently into her house. She screamed.

Coronation Street ist eine der bekanntesten britischen Soap-Operas und spielt in einer fiktiven Stadt in der Nähe von Manchester. Die Serie läuft seit 1960 (gute 25 Jahre länger als die „Lindenstraße"!) und hat auch heute noch mehr als 10 Mio. Zuschauer pro Folge.

"Shut your mouth," snarled the man as he quickly followed her inside and slammed the door shut behind him.
He turned the key, locking the door. It had all taken a matter of seconds. Judith found herself cowering against the hall wall.
"Who are you?" she cried. "What do you want?"
"Get back, bitch," the man snarled.
"Help!" Judith tried to scream, but the man hit her hard in the face.
The force of the blow knocked her to the floor. Katie came bounding in from the kitchen, barking and growling. The little dog flew at the man, her teeth sinking into his shin.
"Argh! Get off, you stupid mutt!" the man shouted as he kicked out at the dog.

to cower	kauern, sich ducken
to bound	springen
⚡ mutt	⚡ Köter
sickening thump	entsetzlicher Knall
to whimper	wimmern
to wrack sth.	etw. erschüttern
jaw	Kiefer
glare	wütender Blick
vice-like	wie ein Schraubstock

Katie flew across the hall and hit the doorframe to the living room with a sickening thump. She whimpered once and was still.
"No! No, no!" Judith screamed.
Violent sobs wracked her body. She was dizzy from the blow and her jaw felt strange.
"Who are you?" she sobbed. "Why are you doing this to me?"
There was no answer. The man simply looked down at her with a hate-filled glare. In desperation Judith tried to crawl away from him, her fingernails digging deep into the thick, beige carpet. But her attacker grabbed her left ankle in a vice-like grip and with an angry grunt, dragged her back.

Exercise 41: Word forms. **Ergänzen Sie das jeweilige Substantiv und Adverb!**

1. uneasy ____________ ____________
2. desperate ____________ ____________
3. angry ____________ ____________
4. violent ____________ ____________
5. strange ____________ ____________

It was half past eleven when James finally walked into the office of *Fans United* the next morning. His clothes were creased and dishevelled. Several of his colleagues noticed his late arrival and looked up from their desks, but James was carefully avoiding meeting anyone's eye. Rob also glanced up as James passed.

That's strange, he thought. It's very late to arrive at work, even for James, and he really does look awful.

James's black hair stood up from his head. He had dark circles under his eyes and he obviously hadn't shaved that morning. With a deep sigh, James put his elbows on the table and rested his face in his hands.

Cathy the receptionist stopped at James's desk with a pile of post.

"Good Morning, James," she said cheerfully but with concern in her voice. "How are you today?"

James gave her a tired and somewhat forced smile.

"Not bad, thanks," he said. "You?"
"I'm okay, I guess. Did you do something exciting last night?"
"Pardon?"
"I…um…I was just wondering if you had done anything exciting last night. You look as if it was a late one."
James gave her a funny look. "You could say that," he eventually replied awkwardly.
Cathy swapped her pile of post into her other arm. Her eyes moved around the room nervously as she tried to think of something else to say or a way to leave without seeming impolite. Rob had a bit of a soft spot for Cathy and so decided to wander over and help her out.
"Hi Cathy. Hello James. Put any more murder victims in your column recently?" he asked jokingly.

creased	zerknittert
dishevelled	unordentlich, ungepflegt
to swap	wechseln, tauschen
ϟ to have a (bit of a) soft spot for sb.	eine (kleine) Schwäche für jmd. haben

"What?" James shouted loudly.
Rob and Cathy stared at him in shock.
"I was just…"
"Just what are you trying to say, Rob?" James interrupted angrily. "It's just a coincidence."
"I, errm…," stuttered Rob.
James stood up suddenly, tipping his chair over. It hit the floor with a crash and the whole office went quiet. Rob was horrified. He felt his cheeks go warm as his colleagues stared at them. James came round from behind his desk and stood nose to nose with Rob, who took a step backwards.
"Well?" said James, pushing Rob in the chest.
"Woah, woah! Calm down, James. It was just a joke, honest."

Exercise 42: Question tags. **Vervollständigen Sie die Sätze mit dem richtigen Frageanhängsel!**

1. James looks terrible, ______________?
2. Everyone noticed James arriving late, ______________?
3. Cathy's always cheerful, ______________?
4. James hadn't shaved, ______________?
5. James won't hit Rob, ______________?

James glared at him before stalking out of the office without a word. He managed to knock into a table by the reception desk and the pile of files stacked on the table slipped to the floor with a crash. By the entrance, he collided with Will and his stationery trolley.

"Careful!" said Will, steadying his trolley.

James marched off without a word or an apology. Will looked into the crowded office and met Rob's eye. He shrugged his shoulders at Rob before continuing on his way.

"Thanks for trying, Rob," whispered Cathy and hurried away with her pile of post.

Embarrassed, Rob slowly made his way back to his own desk. He hid behind the screen of his PC and tried to ignore the stares of his colleagues.

Eventually the noise in the office got back to normal as people returned to their tasks.

to stalk out	hinausmarschieren
to steady sth.	etw. stabilisieren
admittedly	zugegebenermaßen
ϟ over the top	übertrieben
assigned	zugewiesen

What was all that about? wondered Rob. Admittedly his joke hadn't been that funny, but James's reaction was totally over the top. It was obviously just a coincidence that the judge had been murdered after appearing in James's column ... wasn't it? Surely the police must have realized the judge's photo had recently been published in the magazine. Should Rob ring and tell them? They must know. He still felt pretty stupid after contacting them about the homeless man. What would they think if he called again to tell them about a silly article?

Exercise 43: Typical mistakes. Lesen Sie weiter und unterstreichen Sie die richtige Variante!

Rob carried on typing up his notes from Manchester United's last match, but it was **1.** heavy / difficult to concentrate. Just what do I really **2.** know / no about James? Rob **3.** knew / new he could be **4.** violence / violent; the incident in the pub was still very fresh in his mind. Still, it was a big jump from a fight in a pub to thinking James might have **5.** anything / something to do with the judge's **6.** death / dead. It must just be a coincidence...it must be.

Across the city, the incident room at Didsbury police station had emptied slightly. The early morning briefing had finished a couple of hours ago and most of the investigators had left the station to work on their assigned activities. There were people to interview, leads to follow up. The day after a victim was found always meant a heavy workload for everyone. Memories were fresh and there was evidence waiting to be collected and analyzed.

Detective Inspector McKay was studying the notice boards at the front of the incident room. Pages and pages of information, photographs and diagrams had been pinned up as the investigation progressed. Suddenly he turned round to face Chris.

"Poor wee[i] woman."

"Pardon, sir?"

"I was just thinking about Judith Baxter's friend. What was her name? Ivy?"

Sergeant North nodded. Looking up from his notes for a few minutes, he leaned back in his desk chair to listen to his boss.

"What a terrible thing to find your friend murdered like that. Poor wee woman. They had to take her to hospital because she was in shock. We must find this monster. Judith wasn't just killed, she was butchered."

Viele Schotten verwenden regionale Ausdrücke, die Briten aus anderen Landesteilen nicht verwenden. Im Text kommen folgende schottische Ausdrücke vor:

wee	small
dram	a small drink (Schluck)
aye	yes

The crime scene at Judith Baxter's house was one of the worst DI McKay had ever seen. It had taken him several drams of whisky before he could fall asleep the night before.

He continued, "Who is this psycho? No one seems to have noticed him, so he must look very normal. And he has never forced his way into any of his victims' houses, so they either know him or he is very clever. He is very careful. He must stalk his victims first to learn their routines. And these victims aren't random. The way he kills them – this is personal."

Chris twirled his pen between his fingers. "We know that Judge Fitzwilliam-Herbert-Smythe had a link to the coach massacre. So did Greg Summers and Tony Carmichael, but how do Judith Baxter, George Jenkins and Josh Cameron fit in? It doesn't hold together. I've been going through the archived files from the time and haven't found anything yet. But there are still several boxes to go. Some of our officers are scheduled to interview George and Josh's friends and relatives today. We're **drawing a blank** with Judith Baxter, though. We can't find any relatives and her friend Ivy didn't know of any links."

workload	Arbeitsbelastung
to butcher sb.	jmd. abschlachten
random	zufällig
to twirl	drehen
to draw a blank	kein Glück haben, eine Niete ziehen
weary	müde, erschöpft
to be on the verge of sth.	kurz vor etw. stehen

Chris slammed his hand down on his desk in frustration. "The key to this case is here somewhere," he sighed.
Archie agreed. "Aye, we just need to keep looking."
He turned back to the notice boards, a look of concentration on his **weary** face. Chris stared at his computer screen.
I am so sick of this case, he thought. Six people have died in horrific ways and the city **is on the verge of** panic. And we seem to be powerless to stop this killer from striking again.
He suddenly had an idea. Opening up his internet search engine he typed in 'Judith Baxter Manchester United coach massacre' and hit the search button.
"Sir! Look at this!"
Archie came to stand behind Chris. He leaned in closer to read the news article Chris now had on his screen. It had appeared in the *Manchester Evening News* several years ago but it was totally relevant.
"That's it!" he gasped. "We've found our link."
"We knew Judith Baxter was a nurse," said Chris, his face flushed.

"What we didn't know was that she was at the scene on the day of the massacre. This article explains that she was off-duty and watching the match with her husband. It says here, sir, that she helped several of the victims. She saved lives. If this case is to do with the massacre, why would the murderer kill her? She was a heroine."

"I don't know," replied Archie grimly. "But it must be to do with the massacre. It is the thread that ties all of our victims together."

Detective Inspector McKay raised his voice and spoke earnestly to the few remaining officers in the incident room.

Exercise 44: Pronouns. Lesen Sie weiter und unterstreichen Sie alle zehn Personal- und Possessivpronomen!

"If the coach massacre is the link to our serial killer, then we need to move quickly. It is likely that he is already stalking his next victim. We need to know about anyone involved in the coach massacre both on the day and in the years following it."

"Teresa, Chris, your list of potential victims is now our top priority. Make sure everyone has a copy and keep working on it."

"Yes sir," said Chris and Sergeant Marsh together.

Archie spoke loudly and clearly. "I want to know about everyone on that list. What were they doing on the day of the massacre? Where do they live now? Have they noticed anyone following them or behaving suspiciously?"

off-duty	nicht im Dienst
heroine	Heldin
thread	Faden
ϟ brainwave	Geistesblitz
frantically	panisch

Archie turned to the station's newest recruit. "Detective Rasheed!"

"Sir?"

"I want you to take charge of speaking to Josh Cameron and George Jenkins' family and friends. I want to know if they had any link to the massacre, any link at all. Now all of you," he said urgently, "go!"

Chris stood up from his desk. He was putting on his jacket and preparing to leave when he suddenly had a brainwave. He looked again at the name of the article's author and knew he had seen it before. He strode to the notice boards at the front of the room and began frantically leafing through the papers.

"Chris?" asked Archie alarmed.

His sergeant was totally focused. Suddenly he ripped a page from the wall.

"Ah ha!" he exclaimed triumphantly.

He held up a copy of the most recent 'fan of the week' article. The judge's wife had passed it on to him.

"Look at this," he pointed to the column. "James Parker wrote this 'fan of the week' nonsense for *Fans United*. Look at his picture. He was the big, tall fella who was eavesdropping when we visited the magazine."

"And…?"

"And," said Chris, "he also wrote the newspaper article on Judith Baxter!"

"What?" replied Archie in disbelief.

"He wrote them both. Look for yourself. The article on Judith was from years ago. I guess he worked at the *Manchester Evening News* back then. It can't be just another coincidence."
The detective's eyes gleamed with excitement. "Chris, find out where Mr Parker is right now. Then bring him in!"

Exercise 45: Translation quiz. Übersetzen Sie und enträtseln Sie das Lösungswort!

1. Reisebus ☐ _ _ _ _
2. lauschen _ _ _ _ _ _ _ ☐ _
3. Krankenhaus _ _ _ _ ☐ _ _ _
4. Krankenschwester ☐ _ _ _ _
5. verdächtig _ _ _ _ _ ☐ _ _ _ _
6. Geistesblitz _ _ _ ☐ _ _ _ _ _ _
7. Faden _ _ _ _ _ ☐
8. Suchmaschine _ _ _ _ _ _ ☐ _ _ _ _ _
9. Unsinn _ _ ☐ _ _ _ _ _ _
10. Rekrut _ _ ☐ _ _ _ _
11. Heldin _ ☐ _ _ _ _ _ _

Lösung: ☐ ☐ ☐ ☐ ☐ ☐ ☐ ☐ ☐ ☐ ☐

Rob decided to leave the office for his lunch hour rather than eat at his desk as he often did. He met his editor Kevin at the main door.

to gleam	funkeln, glitzern
to bring sb. in	*hier*: jmd. zur Vernehmung bringen
cubicle	Kabine
façade	Fassade, Anschein

"Just going out, Rob?"
"Yes, I thought I'd get some daylight and stretch my legs."
"Good idea."
They walked down the steps to the street together. It wasn't just the need for some exercise that had made Rob leave his desk. Since his encounter with James, he'd had problems concentrating. He hoped a change of scenery would help.
"Kevin, did you see James this morning?" he asked his editor.
"Only when he was making his dramatic exit. He looked absolutely awful. Woman troubles, I expect," Kevin chuckled. "Just ignore him."
"Oh, I see. Oh dear," said Rob thoughtfully.

The killer stared at his reflection in the mirror. His colleagues were elsewhere in the office and he had the toilets and cubicles to himself. His eyes were wild and staring. He felt as if his crimes were written all over his face. He had come so, so close to losing control that morning. He ran his hands through his hair which was sticking out madly from his head.
I even look crazy, he thought.
He had never killed a woman before. Somehow it had been different. It felt different. Killing her had definitely been the right thing to do, but for some reason he couldn't get Judith's death out of his head. Killing the others hadn't bothered him, but her screams echoed continuously in his mind. It was difficult to focus on anything and maintain his façade of normality.

Exercise 46: Multiple Choice. **Welcher Satz ist korrekt? Kreuzen Sie an!**

1. The editor thinks James is angry because...
   a) ❐ of relationship problems.
   b) ❐ he has lost some money.

2. When the massacre happened, Judith...
   a) ❐ was first on the scene.
   b) ❐ gave first aid to the victims.

3. The police think James Parker is a suspect because...
   a) ❐ he was there when the coach massacre happened.
   b) ❐ two victims appeared in articles he wrote.

4. Sergeant North got the most recent 'fan of the week' article from...
   a) ❐ the judge's wife.
   b) ❐ the judge's office.

5. Rob went out at lunchtime because...
   a) ❐ he wanted some exercise.
   b) ❐ he couldn't concentrate.

"Just breathe," he said to himself, taking slow, deep breaths. "Just breathe."

to stoke	anfachen
willpower	Willenskraft

It was so difficult to spend every day in the same office with Rob. Rob's every word stoked the fire of hatred inside him. It took every atom of willpower to pretend that he was fine and happy. At times it felt as if his anger was going to burst out of him.

Exercise 47: Translation. Lesen Sie weiter und unterstreichen Sie die englische Übersetzung der angegebenen Begriffe!

versteckt | übte | Geheimnis | Trost | Rache

His only comfort came from knowing that his knife was hidden carefully in his bag. Just thinking about it gave him a thrill. It was his secret. He could take it out at a moment's notice and take his revenge. He needed to be careful, though. He needed to be clever and keep hidden. Straightening his clothes and flattening his hair, the killer practised his smile in the mirror.

"Hi!" he said confidently.
That would do, he thought. He looked normal. No one would ever know. He was not done yet.

7 SO CLOSE...

The elderly man was slumped in the corner of his armchair, his white hair surrounding his head like a cloud.

God, this is depressing, thought Sergeant North as he looked around. I hope I never end up in a care home.

Various ancient residents were propped up in comfortable chairs round the edges of the communal living room. Some were dribbling, most were asleep. Nurses kept popping their heads around the door. Checking that no one is having any fun, thought Chris gloomily. We need to get out of here as soon as possible.

elderly	ältere(r), ältlich
to slump	zusammensinken
care home	Pflegeheim
communal	gemeinschaftlich
to dribble	sabbern
to jolt awake	aus dem Schlaf hochschrecken
dressing gown	Bademantel
radio	*hier*: Funk
surveillance	Überwachung

"Detective Evans," he said loudly. "Stuart!"

The old man jolted awake again. He peered at Sergeant North and Detective Inspector McKay out of confused, blue eyes. His red dressing gown was loose on his frame and stained with remains of his breakfast.

Chris looked at his boss for help.

"Detective Evans," said Archie gently, "you were telling us about the day of the coach massacre, sir."

Exercise 48: Verb forms. **Lesen Sie weiter und setzen Sie die Verben in der richtigen Form in die passende Lücke!**

run happen hear evacuate say reach

"Yes, yes!" 1. ______ the retired policeman excitedly, 2. ______ for his glass of water with a trembling hand. "I was working on the south side of the stadium when the shooting 3. ______. We 4. ______ the shots of course. Then we were told on the radio 5. ______ the grounds as quickly as possible. I 6. ______ to the gates to help. We needed to avoid a mass panic..."

Archie was listening with an interested expression on his face but his mind was elsewhere. James Parker had already left the *Fans United* offices when he and Sergeant North had arrived the afternoon before. Parker hadn't returned to his flat last night either. The police officers who visited his home had spoken to his rather upset, now ex-girlfriend.

"I haven't seen him," she snapped. "We had a row last night and he pushed me. I've finally had enough. I hope he never comes back!"

Archie had arranged for a surveillance team to wait outside the flat for Parker to come back. The officers had been there all night. In the meantime, all patrol cars had been given Parker's descrip-

available	verfügbar
maze	Labyrinth
ϟ pig	ϟ Bulle
viciously	boshaft, gemein

tion and would be looking for him. Archie was hopeful it was only a matter of time before he was found. While they waited, all available teams were interviewing people who had been at the stadium on the day of the coach massacre. They were trying to build up a picture of what it had been like on the day and who their killer could be.

"...Do you remember a Detective Carmichael? He was on the force at the same time as you," asked DI McKay.

"Ah yes," said Stuart grimly. "I remember Tony. I never liked the man. There was something about him. You never felt he was being totally honest with you."

"What do you mean?" asked Archie.

They were interrupted by the ringing of Sergeant North's mobile phone.

"Sorry, I'll just get this," he said as he got up to take the call in the hall.

"What were you saying about Tony Carmichael?" asked Archie, turning back to the old man, but he had fallen asleep again.

Archie sighed heavily. This was such a waste of time!

Seconds later Chris burst back into the room and gestured at his boss. With a final glance at the sleeping ex-policeman, Archie crossed the room to join his sergeant.

"James Parker has been spotted in Chorlton!" whispered Chris.

Detective Inspector McKay and Sergeant North raced across the city with their sirens blaring. The Chorlton area of Manchester was a maze of shops and old houses which had been turned into cheap flats. Chris had to wind the car through the little streets filled with pedestrians and students on bikes.

"Move! Move!" Sergeant North shouted, thumping the steering wheel in frustration.
"Fill me in, Chris," instructed Archie. "Where exactly was James Parker seen?"
Sergeant North didn't take his eyes off the road. "A pair of officers on foot patrol recognized him and called for back-up. They were following him when he went into his girlfriend's salon. She's a hairdresser. Apparently he began by shouting and screaming threats at her, then he started throwing stuff around. That's when the manager called us."
They rounded a corner and Sergeant North brought the car to an abrupt stop behind a police van.
"I guess this is the back-up!" he said.
The two men leapt from the vehicle. They could see James Parker by the smashed window of a hairdressing salon. He was shouting and gesturing wildly at four uniformed police officers who were trying to both calm him down and keep the gathering crowd at a safe distance.
"Stay back, pigs!" screamed James viciously.
He was holding a pair of sharp scissors[i] tightly in his right hand and was pointing the blades at anyone who came too close. One of the police officers recognized DI McKay and came to meet him.
"Hello, sir. I hear you've been looking for this chap. The staff managed to push him outside and lock the door before we got here. Un-

Plural Nouns
Eine Gruppe von englischen Nomen wird nur im Plural verwendet. Dazu gehören die Dinge, die aus 2 identischen Teilen bestehen wie **scissors, glasses, trousers, jeans, pyjamas, tights** und **binoculars:**
z.B. *My pyjamas are red.*
Um eine genaue Anzahl anzugeben, ergänzt man die Mengenangabe **a pair of:**
z.B. *She has a new pair of glasses.*
I bought two pairs of jeans today.

to fan out	ausschwärmen
scuffling	raufend
to restrain sb.	jmd. bändigen
to catch sb. off guard	jmd. überrumpeln

fortunately he managed to grab some of their scissors on his way out. He's also smashed that window," he gestured behind him.
"Okay, thank you, PC Errington," said DI McKay grimly. "Let's go and talk to him, Chris."

Exercise 49: Definitions. Ordnen Sie den Wörtern die passende Definition zu!

1. ☐ honest	a) to move your hands or head to show what you mean
2. ☐ steering wheel	b) an angry argument
3. ☐ to gesture	c) a person travelling on foot
4. ☐ pedestrian	d) always telling the truth
5. ☐ row	e) what a driver uses to decide direction

The Detective Inspector carefully approached James, his hands open by his side in a non-threatening way. The other officers fanned out around their suspect.
"Hello, Mr Parker," said Archie calmly. "We'd like to talk to you. Can you put down the scissors please, sir."
"I said get back!" James snarled.
He leapt towards the DI. As he did so, Sergeant North and PC Errington moved in and wrestled James to the ground. James dropped the scissors, which DI McKay quickly kicked away.

Two of the other officers came to the aid of the scuffling men on the floor. James Parker was throwing wild punches and roaring in fury. It took all four policemen to restrain him and get him into the back of the waiting police van.
"Are you okay, son?" asked DI McKay.
PC Errington had been caught by one of James's fists and was clearly going to develop a painful-looking black eye.
"Ouch!" sympathised Chris.
PC Errington grimaced. "I'm alright. He just caught me off guard."
"Right, let's get Mr Parker back to the station," DI McKay said. "He has some serious questions to answer."

Exercise 50: Translation. Lesen Sie weiter und übersetzen Sie den Abschnitt ins Deutsche!

That evening, Rob and Dave met in the Didsbury Arms, their favourite pub in South Manchester, to watch the Wednesday night match. Manchester United was playing in Munich.
Rob returned from the bar with two pints of beer and a couple of packets of peanuts.

____

____

____

____

____

____

____

rowdy	rüpelhaft, wild
sociable	gesellig
↯ to be miles away	mit den Gedanken ganz woanders sein
to insist	bestehen auf
staple	Heftklammer
the implication was that	man konnte daraus schließen, dass …
to be on edge	nervös sein
brooding	grüblerisch

"Cheers, mate," said Dave, taking a sip of his pint.

This evening the pub was busy but not too overcrowded. They'd arrived early and had managed to secure a table near the television screen. A group of rowdy students had claimed the neighbouring table. Their loud laughter was beginning to get on Rob's nerves. If he was honest, Rob wasn't really in the mood for watching football or being sociable. Usually his attention was totally absorbed by a match, but tonight he couldn't concentrate.

"So tell me what's happened with that colleague of yours," said Dave. "It's all over the news. The police have finally arrested someone in connection with the serial killings. I can't believe you have been working with a murderer!"

"Neither can I," said Rob gloomily.

Cathy, the receptionist, had been the first to tell Rob the news when he arrived at the office that morning.

"Rob, have you heard about James?" she'd gasped. "He's been arrested. The police think he is the serial killer."

Dave waved his hand in front of Rob's face, who was miles away as he remembered the shock of hearing the news for the first time.

"Hellooooo, Rob. Didn't you guess?" asked Dave, eager for details. "Weren't there any clues?"

Rob had been asking himself the same questions, but there had been nothing specific that had marked James out as a potential serial killer. And yet, hadn't he thought there was something odd? Maybe he should have rung the police about Judge Maximillian Fitzwilliam-Herbert-Smythe appearing in James's article. Would it have saved the latest victim? Did Rob have blood on his hands now because he hadn't called?

"Well, come on!" insisted Dave. "The most exciting thing that happened to me today was running out of staples!"

Rob smiled weakly. He felt strangely empty. All the newspaper reports had said how 'police were talking to a person of interest in the serial killer investigation.' The implication was that the killer had been caught. The city had been on edge for weeks now, and there was a sense of relief in the pub tonight. He was pleased that the murderer had finally been captured. However, Rob didn't know how to react now he knew the killer was James. He also couldn't shake off a feeling of unease. Several times during the day Rob had felt as if he was being watched.

"It was all everyone could talk about in the office today," Rob said finally.

No official announcement had been made, but somehow the news had spread. The mood in the office had been very odd. It was awful to think that they had all been sitting near and working so closely to a murderer.

"It was strange really," added Rob. "Everyone was talking about why they thought James had done it. It was as if he'd already been found guilty. No one had anything nice to say about him, even the people I thought were his friends. It's as if they were all trying to distance themselves from him."

Rob fell into a brooding silence. Going into the canteen at lunchtime, he had heard all sorts of horrible comments from his colleagues about James. And even friendly Cathy had said, "I always thought there was something dangerous about him."

Exercise 51: Crossword puzzle. Lösen Sie das Kreuzworträtsel!

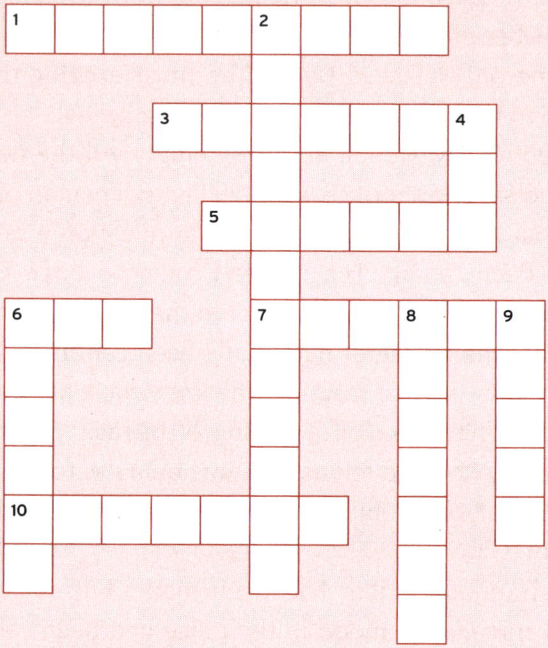

Across

1. someone you work with
3. a restaurant in a workplace
5. a loud, cheerful laugh
6. the opposite of happy
7. a pair
10. a person who is learning

Down

2. a public statement
4. just at this moment
6. If you have too much to do, you experience...
8. a common bar snack
9. precise

Rob didn't like James himself, but he'd been shocked by how quickly his workmates had turned on one of their own. Dave put his hand dramatically on Rob's arm and looked at him with an overly serious expression on his face.

"With this nasty man off the streets, do you think Susan will let you out alone again?"

Rob managed to keep a straight face for a couple of seconds before breaking out into a loud guffaw. He felt the stress of the past few days begin to lift.

workmate	Arbeitskollege
to turn on sb.	sich gegen jmd. wenden, auf jmd. losgehen
to keep a straight face	ernst bleiben, sich das Lachen verkneifen
guffaw	schallendes Gelächter
subdued	gedämpft, düster
fruitless	erfolglos
to charge with criminal damage and assault	anklagen wegen Sachbeschädigung und Körperverletzung

"Thanks, pal," he smiled. "That's exactly what I needed."

Rob took a long drink of his beer. On the television screen, Manchester United's striker was brought down by a tackle near the opposition's goal. This time Rob was on his feet with the rest of the pub.

"Oh come on, referee!"

Twenty-four hours later, the incident room at Didsbury Police Station was quiet and subdued. The excitement and hope which had come with James Parker's arrest the day before had gone. After a long and fruitless evening and day spent questioning James, the police had been forced to let him go.

"Well, it's official. Mr Parker has been charged with criminal damage and assault on both his girlfriend and the officer who arrested him," said Detective Inspector McKay. "He has been

to release sb. on bail	jmd. gegen Kaution frei-lassen
confession	Geständnis
prime suspect	Hauptver-dächtiger
dimly	dunkel, schwach
bolt upright	kerzengerade

released on bail so he has to report to the station every two days. I have arranged a surveillance team to watch him twenty-four hours a day, so at least we'll know where he is."

Sergeant North was exhausted. He was slumped at his desk, a mug of strong coffee in front of him. His boss was leaning against a table in the middle of the room and facing him.

"I suppose so," said Chris. "Without an obvious motive, any forensic evidence linking him to the murder scenes or a confession, we couldn't hold him any longer."

"He's still our prime suspect, though," added DI McKay.

The incident room was dimly lit and almost empty. Only the officers on the night shift were at their desks. Everyone else had gone home feeling depressed and fearful. They knew the serial killer was still out on the streets. The Chief Inspector[i] had given a press conference a couple of hours earlier and announced that their only suspect had been released. The panic in the room had been noticeable. Archie could only imagine the headlines on the evening's news reports.

Berufsbezeichnungen wie **Chief Inspector** (Hauptkommissar) sowie Titel werden im Englischen nur großgeschrieben, wenn sie als Anrede oder Teil eines Namens verwendet werden. In allen anderen Fällen werden sie kleingeschrieben.
Z.B. *The inspector went back to his desk.*
Rob greeted Sergeant North.

"We should head home," he said wearily. "It's been a long day."

"I know, sir, but somehow it feels like admitting defeat."

Exercise 52: Possessive pronouns. Lesen Sie weiter und ergänzen Sie die richtigen Possessivpronomen!

Detective Inspector McKay rubbed **1.** ______ eyes with his hands. "I know, son, I know. Right, if we're here, let's make our time count. Sergeant Marsh and **2.** ______ team left **3.** ______ report on **4.** ______ desk earlier," he continued. "I found it when we returned from the interview room earlier. Teresa has spent the day speaking with relatives of **5.** ______ victims."

"And?" Chris asked.
"Both George Jenkins and Josh Cameron were there on the day of the coach massacre."
"No way!" Chris sat bolt upright in his chair.
"Before he became a lorry driver, George Jenkins was a coach driver."
"He was driving the coach that day?" guessed Chris.
"Correct. And there was speculation at the time that he may have slowed down to let the gunmen on board. He was shot in the leg during the gunfight, but the suspicion followed him for years."
Chris was speechless. How had this been missed before?
"What about Josh Cameron?" he asked.
"Well, this link is a bit weaker. Josh's mum was still very upset about what happened. Josh was only nineteen on the day of the massacre. He was working in the car park, directing and control-

puzzle	Rätsel
to catch one's eye	jmd. ins Auge fallen
marshal	*hier*: Ordner, Platzwart
↯ Yuck!	Igitt!
alert	Alarm

ling the exit gate for pedestrians. The gunmen escaped through his gate. He got a lot of criticism from people at the time for letting the gunmen escape. Goodness only knows why. They had weapons and he was only nineteen, for God's sake!"

"What did they expect him to have done?"

"Exactly," the Detective Inspector continued thoughtfully. "The massacre must be the link between all the murders. We just need to work out why."

Chris was silent for a moment. "But why Judith?" he finally asked, thinking aloud. "You could argue that the others all helped the gunmen in some way, but she helped the victims. Her murder doesn't make any sense."

"Yes," replied Archie. "Our killer could be a victim or a relative. He could also be a gangland killer looking for revenge for Michael Sullivan's murder."

"Yes, but Judith Baxter doesn't fit," insisted Chris. "She went onto the coach to give first aid to the victims. She put herself in danger. Judith had no way of knowing who had guns and if the attackers were still on the coach or not. Whichever way you look at it, Mrs Baxter does not fit in this pattern."

"Then maybe she is the key to this **puzzle**," suggested Archie. "She did appear in an article by James Parker. So did the judge. Maybe that's how James chose his victims?"

"We've not found any of the others in his articles, though," replied Chris. "Plus, you saw him outside the hairdressing salon. He was totally out of control. I don't see how he can be our cold, calculating serial killer."

"So if it's not James, then who is it?"
"God, I wish we knew!" said Chris, raising his arms in frustration and accidentally knocking over the pile of papers on his desk. The sheets flew everywhere. Cursing, he began to pick them up until one of the sheets suddenly caught his eye.
"Hang on a minute, sir. This is the list of all the people we could find that were involved in the coach massacre on the day or since. We have passengers, victims, their relatives, police, reporters, marshals, staff at snack food stands...everyone we could think of. Teresa must have finished it today and left it on my desk."

Exercise 53: Prepositions. Lesen Sie weiter und ergänzen Sie die Sätze mit den passenden Präpositionen!

Chris handed the list **1.** ________ his boss. The Detective Inspector sighed and took a sip **2.** ________ his now cold coffee. Yuck!
DI McKay began to read, looking **3.** ________ familiar names.
"Bingo!" he shouted, thrusting the list at Chris. "Recognize him?"
Chris nodded.
"Send **4.** ________ an alert to all officers and grab your coat. If this is our killer, we must find him immediately. Looking **5.** ________ the time between his other victims, he will be getting ready to kill again!"

to draw to a close	sich dem Ende zuneigen
bustling	belebt, geschäftig
line	*hier*: Kollektion
aimlessly	ziellos
soothing	beruhigend, entspannend
insistent	hartnäckig
↯ to die	*hier*: ausgehen
↯ hun (honey)	Schatz
debris	Abfälle, Überbleibsel

Across the city, the evening's event at Old Trafford was drawing to a close. Manchester United's management had decided to host a reception for *Fans United* and other fan publications.

"As if champagne is going to stop us writing about them when they've done something wrong," snorted Kevin, the editor, still bitter about the team's defeat the night before.

Rob nodded. He was exhausted after the drama of the last few days and the event had run on far later than expected. He needed to ring Susan and let her know he'd be late. Rob excused himself and left the brightly-lit, bustling function room.

"Hello, lovely. Sorry if I woke you up," he said when she answered. "I'll be home soon. I can't wait to see you."

She yawned. "Don't worry. I'm just on my way to bed. Long evening?" she asked sympathetically.

"Just a bit! Anyway, tell me about your day…"

Susan launched into a long description of the argument she'd had with her manager about the latest line in clothing he'd purchased for the company. Rob wandered around aimlessly as he listened, happy to let her talk. The sound of her voice and the ordinariness of her day's events were soothing after his stressful few days.

An insistent beeping eventually interrupted their conversation.

"Oh dear," said Rob. "The battery on my mobile is about to die."

"Okay, hun," Susan replied sleepily. "See you later."

"Hopefully I won't be long. Bye for now. Love you."
Rob hung up and slipped the phone into his jacket pocket. He suddenly became aware that he had wandered into an unknown part of the stadium.
He made his way back to the function room as quickly as he could. When he finally got there, it seemed too quiet. Rob opened the door and gasped. It was empty! The lights were off and the used glasses and debris of the evening had been left for the next morning. He must have been talking to Susan for longer than he'd realized.

Exercise 54: Opposites. Welches Wort bedeutet das Gegenteil? Kreuzen Sie an!

1. win
   a) ☐ victory
   b) ☐ defeat
   c) ☐ triumph

2. exhausted
   a) ☐ very tired
   b) ☐ worn out
   c) ☐ refreshed

3. soothing
   a) ☐ calming
   b) ☐ stressful
   c) ☐ relaxing

4. unknown
   a) ☐ familiar
   b) ☐ strange
   c) ☐ foreign

5. deserted
   a) ☐ bustling
   b) ☐ empty
   c) ☐ abandoned

to plunge into	(ein)tauchen in
concrete	Beton
to lose one's bearings	die Orientierung verlieren

Rob rushed down to the main door where he'd entered the stadium earlier. It was locked! Suddenly all the lights went off and the stadium was plunged into darkness. Rob's heart began to pound in his chest.

"Calm down, you idiot," he muttered to himself. "It's just dark."

He took his phone from his pocket to call Kevin or Susan. They could arrange for someone to come and let him out. The phone's screen was blank. The battery was completely dead. This was so embarrassing.

Someone must still be in the building, surely, thought Rob. I just need to find them.

Walking quickly, he hurried down a corridor that he knew led towards the team changing rooms and the tunnels onto the pitch.

"Hello?" he called as he went. "Can you help me, please? I'm locked in!"

Rob walked through a set of double doors and then another. Each dark corridor looked identical – closed, locked doors and grey concrete floors. Rob soon lost his bearings and he began to feel a little panicked.

Stop being ridiculous, he told himself. I'll find a way out. At the very worst, I'll set the alarm off and the police will come and find me. It'll be embarrassing but at least I'll be out.

Suddenly Rob stopped. He was sure he could hear footsteps behind him. He listened again.

"Hello? Who's there?" he called loudly.

Silence… The hairs began to stand up on the back of Rob's neck.

8 A CHANCE TO KILL

The killer had been watching Rob all evening. Despite the noise and crowds in the room, Rob's presence had drawn him like a magnet. Even when the killer had been talking to other guests, he had always known where Rob was. The room had been set out specially for the evening's event. Champagne flowed from the bar near the door and tables at the other end were set with the usual buffet, which had attracted a steady crowd all evening.

A few minutes ago, Kevin Skinner had wandered back from the buffet for the second time with an overloaded plate and given him a wink.

"Not bad, eh? Don't tell the wife!"

The killer had given him the obligatory chuckle, but he felt curiously cold and detached. He could see people chatting and enjoying themselves, but it was as if there was some invisible barrier between them and him. It felt as if he was inside a bubble.

detached	distanziert, unbeteiligt
⚡ Whoopsie!	⚡ Uups!

"Excuse me, dear."

The killer stepped aside to let a middle-aged lady pass by him. The evening was drawing to a close and she had obviously had too much to drink. She grabbed his arm to steady herself.

"Whoopsie!"

Exercise 55: Translation. Lesen Sie weiter und übersetzen Sie die markierten Satzteile!

The killer put a fixed smile on his face but **1.** in ihm brannte sein Hass ______________________.
Why should he be forced to put up with this nonsense and these stupid, weak people? **2.** Er lächelte in sich hinein ______________________. If these idiots only knew what thoughts were running through his head! **3.** Er war so gelangweilt ______________________ of making small talk all evening and didn't know how much longer he could keep smiling.
So when he saw Rob slip out of the room, he decided to follow. Perhaps he would finally get an opportunity to strike.
The killer crept along quietly behind Rob. **4.** Der Partylärm ______________________ faded into the background.

The killer took care to hide in the shadows of the dimly-lit corridors and keep close to the walls. He hung back at corners, always able to hear Rob but not necessarily to see him. However, he soon realized that he didn't need to be so careful.
"Uh huh…okay, Susan,…yep…"

flick knife	Klappmesser
invincible	unbesiegbar

Rob was totally absorbed in his phone call and didn't notice his stalker. Excellent! The killer couldn't believe his luck. He fingered the edge of the flick knife he always kept hidden in his pocket. Just the touch of it gave him a thrill. He was powerful; he was invincible.

"Really? Good for you, Susan," said Rob into his mobile.

The corridors of the stadium were like a maze, and as he wandered Rob was becoming more and more isolated from the rest of the party. The killer hadn't planned to strike tonight, but maybe this was an opportunity too good to be missed.

"Come on, Anderson, keep walking," he muttered to himself.

He stopped as Rob paused briefly before taking a staircase that led down to the ground floor and into the labyrinth of changing rooms, store rooms, offices and gyms around the edge of the pitch. His excitement grew as he realized that he might be able to get rid of Rob forever tonight!

This is it, he thought. This is my opportunity!

He pulled the knife out and flicked open the blade. Now I just need to wait for the right moment…

Bang, bang!

Sergeant North thumped loudly on the flat door.

"This is the police. Sir, open up!" he shouted.

No answer.

"Knock again, Chris," said Detective Inspector McKay.

Both detectives were on their guard. Despite the well-lit, bright staircase and smartly-painted doors, they could be standing just feet away from their killer. Sergeant North banged noisily on the door again.

obese	fettleibig
↯ racket	Krach, Lärm
tracksuit bottoms *pl*	Jogginghosen
to poke out	hervorgucken
landlord	Vermieter
petulantly	verdrossen
to hitch up	hochziehen
plain	einfach, unscheinbar
subtle	*hier*: klein; subtil

"Sir, open up!"

There was still no answer.

"Enough," said DI McKay. "Kick the door down, Chris."

At that moment, the door to the next flat flew open and an obese, middle-aged man came hurrying out.

"Woah, woah, woah! What's this racket about? Don't you know what time it is? Hang on a minute! Don't go kicking anything down. That's my door!"

"I beg your pardon?"

"That's my door!" insisted the man. "I'm Neil Edmonton. I own the flat."

He had grey, slightly greasy hair that was a bit too long at the back. He was wearing tracksuit bottoms and slippers. His fat, pale belly was poking out from under his green T-shirt.

"Do you know the man who lives here?" asked Sergeant North.

"Of course I do," the man replied indignantly. "I rent the flat to him. What's going on? Is he okay?"

"Have you seen him this evening?" asked Chris.

"Why do you ask?"

"Sir, have you seen him? Answer the question, please," commanded the sergeant and held up his police badge.

The landlord looked at them petulantly.

For goodness sake! thought Detective Inspector McKay in frustration.

"Mr Edmonton," he insisted. "Can you let us into the flat, please? It's very important."

The landlord looked at them suspiciously. "Well…I'm not sure."

Exercise 56: Definitions match-up. **Ordnen Sie den Wörtern die passende Definition zu!**

1. ☐ landlord	a) to move slowly, quietly and carefully
2. ☐ invincible	b) very fat
3. ☐ labyrinth	c) cannot be beaten or defeated
4. ☐ creep	d) a man who rents out property he owns
5. ☐ obese	e) a complex network of passages

"Sir," DI McKay said seriously, "we need to get into that flat. It could be a matter of life and death."

Neil **hitched up** his trousers and sighed. "Fine, I'll get the key."

The two policemen exchanged frustrated looks as Mr Edmonton went back into his flat. He was back in a couple of minutes and unlocked the door to their suspect's flat.

"Please wait here, sir," Chris told the landlord.

The two policemen turned the lights on as they entered the flat. It was fairly **plain** but modern-looking with shiny wooden floors and cream walls. They entered the first room on the right. It was a bedroom, tidy and impersonal, with no photographs or ornaments. There was nothing to give an impression of what kind of person lived there.

"What are we looking for, sir?" asked Sergeant North.

"I'm not sure exactly," replied DI McKay as he peered into the wardrobe. "Look for anything that will tell us where our suspect is or any clues that he could be our killer. It could be very **subtle**."

Sergeant North left his boss searching the bedroom and went into the living room.

Exercise 57: Correct the mistakes. Lesen Sie weiter und korrigieren Sie die sechs Fehler im folgenden Absatz!

The room had large windows and basic furnitures: a table, armchairs, a television and bookcase. However, this was not what catched Sergeant Norths immediate attention.
"Oh my God!" he gasped. "Sir! Come quick!"
DI McKay hurried into the living room and his mouth felt open in shock as he looking around the room.

1. ____________________ 4. ____________________

2. ____________________ 5. ____________________

3. ____________________ 6. ____________________

"He's definitely our man," said Chris with a relieved sigh.
As awful as the scene was, he felt strangely happy that finally they had found their killer.
"It looks that way," murmured Archie.
He couldn't take his eyes away from the display in front of him. On the wall directly opposite the door were a series of large photographs. Even though they were incredibly defaced, the policemen could instantly recognize the faces of their six vic-

defaced	verunstaltet
mutilated	verstümmelt

tims. In the photographs the victims were full of life and smiling, not the images of horrifically mutilated bodies the policemen had become so familiar with. But this alone hadn't caused their shock.

"Have you ever seen anything like this before?" asked Chris.

"Not even close, thankfully," replied Archie.

Exercise 58: Word spiral. Finden Sie die Begriffe und füllen Sie die Wortspirale!

1	2	3	4	5	6	7	8
22	23	24	25	26	27	28	9
21	36	37	38	39	40	29	10
20	35	34	33	32	31	30	11
19	18	17	16	15	14	13	12

1-5: very fat

5-16: When you do something really stupid in front of other people, it's...

16-25: what you get on your skin when you are cold or scared

25-28: a short, quiet breath when you are sad or frustrated

28-34: a very brave woman

34-40: an investigation to find answers

The awful photo montage in front of them gave a terrifying insight into the mind of the killer. The eyes of the victims in each photograph had been obliterated by angry, black marks. Deep slash marks and hateful words had been carved into the wall around the pictures:

MURDERER, BETRAYER, GUILTY, DIE!

"Oh shit!" Neil Edmonton's voice behind them startled the two men.

"Sir, you can't be in here," said DI McKay. "It's a crime scene."

to obliterate	auslöschen, tilgen
to get hold of sth.	*hier*: herankommen an
to pray	beten
renewed purpose	neuer Elan

"But..."

Sergeant North led the man out of the apartment, using his body to try and block the landlord's view. The last thing they needed was the press getting hold of the details.

"He's gone and I've locked the door," said Chris coming back into the room.

"Good," said DI McKay, gesturing at the wall. "I've reported it to the station. Back-up and a forensics teams are on their way. Every available officer is out looking for our suspect. We need to find him before he knows we've identified him."

Sergeant North headed towards the living room door, intent on searching the rest of the flat.

"Hang on, Chris," said DI McKay slowly. "There are seven photographs."

"But we only have six victims," Chris added.

The two men crossed the living room to look more closely at the one remaining, unmarked photo. To their amazement they recognized the face.

"That's Rob Anderson!" exclaimed Sergeant North.

"Find him," said DI McKay grimly. "And start praying we're not too late."

At the stadium, Rob stopped. He held his breath and listened. Nothing.

He was sure he had heard footsteps behind him just a moment ago. However, if there was someone else in the building, they had also paused.

Very strange, thought Rob, feeling more and more nervous. If there is someone else there, why don't they make themselves known?

"Hello?" Rob called again. "Is anyone there?"

Silence.

He could feel fear beginning to take hold of his nerves. This is ridiculous, Rob told himself. I am imagining things. It's late. I need to find a way out, go home, kiss Susan and go to sleep. There must be an exit somewhere nearby.

Rob set off with **renewed purpose**. But suddenly he heard a noise behind him. There was definitely someone else in the stadium and someone who wanted to remain hidden. Rob began to run. He needed to get out.

Exercise 59: Tense markers. Setzen Sie die angegebenen Signalwörter richtig ein!

before ago yesterday since for

1. The massacre took place 16 years ______.
2. I haven't seen him ______ yesterday.
3. Have you ever seen anything like this ______?
4. The police have been looking for him ______ hours.
5. He didn't come home ______.

to rev the engine	den Motor aufheulen lassen
to kick in	anspringen, sich einschalten
landline	Festnetz
reassuringly	beruhigend
↯ worth a shot	einen Versuch wert

Detective Inspector McKay fastened his seatbelt as Sergeant North revved the engine of the patrol car. He roared away from the killer's block of flats with the sirens blaring, his headlights cutting through the dark. The two policemen were headed towards Rob and Susan's flat. Other officers would meet them there. Until this maniac was found, they needed to get Rob Anderson into police protection.

"Faster, Chris! Faster!" Archie almost shouted.

Leafing through his notebook, the DI found where he'd scribbled down Rob's mobile number after their interview. He punched in the numbers. It rang a few times and then the voicemail kicked in. The DI cursed. As the car flew round corners, he tried Rob's landline number.

"Come on, come on!" he urged as the phone rang again.

This time, a sleepy voice answered on the third ring.

"Hello?"

"Susan? This is Detective Inspector McKay. Is Rob with you?"

"What? No!" she was suddenly very awake. "What's wrong? Has something happened to him?"

"No, not as far as we know," replied Archie reassuringly. "But we need to find him. We think he might be in danger."

"Oh God! Rob isn't here. He was at an evening event at Old Trafford with the magazine. He called me half an hour ago."

"Chris, head to the stadium, as quick as you can," ordered DI McKay.

As Chris swung the car around, the Detective Inspector spoke urgently to the worried woman on the other end of the phone.

Exercise 60: Modal verbs. Lesen Sie weiter und unterstreichen Sie die richtige Variante!

"Susan, listen to me. This is very important. Stay in the flat and lock all the doors. I **1.** shall / should send some officers round to wait with you. You **2.** may / must not open the door until you have seen their ID. And try not to worry, we **3.** would / will find Rob."

"I understand," she sobbed. "Please find him."

"You **4.** could / must try ringing the *Fans United* office, Archie," suggested Sergeant North. "They **5.** can / may be able to contact someone at the event who knows where Rob is."

"It's late but definitely worth a shot."
DI McKay scrolled through his phone and dialled the number.
The phone rang and rang.
"Damn it!" cursed DI McKay. "There's no one there. I don't like this, Chris. We're still several miles from the football stadium. I'm calling for back-up. I want all available units to head to the stadium. Let's hope we're not too late."

There was no mistaking the sound of footsteps this time. Rob broke into a run. He was really scared now. Someone was definitely following him, someone who would not identify themselves.

momentum	Schwung, Wucht
assailant	Angreifer
to glisten	(feucht) glänzen

"Help!" shouted Rob. "Let me out!"

He heard his pursuer's running footsteps getting closer. Rob had reached the top of a staircase. He paused briefly, panting. Which way should he go?

Suddenly he was hit from behind and he felt a terrible, overwhelming pain in his left shoulder.

"Argh!"

Instinctively Rob lurched to one side. It wasn't what his attacker had been expecting and as Rob moved, his attacker's **momentum** carried him forwards and head-first down the stairs. Rob didn't wait to see if his **assailant** was injured. Clutching his shoulder, Rob fled; blood was pumping out between his fingers.

He ran as fast as he could, twisting and turning through the maze of corridors. Desperate, Rob sprinted down another corridor and threw himself against the door at the end. It was locked! He pulled frantically at the handle, smearing it with his blood.

Rob turned. "No!"

A shadowy figure had turned the corner and was slowly approaching him down the corridor. Rob backed up against the locked door. He was breathing hard, his left arm hung uselessly against his side, and blood was dripping from his sleeve to the floor.

"Stay away!" he screamed, terrified.

The dark figure came closer with each slow step. His bloodied blade **glistened** in the little light available in the corridor. Then the man's face became visible.

"Will?" gasped Rob in shock. "You! Why are you here?"

The killer smiled evilly. "To kill you. Isn't it obvious?"

Exercise 61: Questions about the text. **Beantworten Sie die Fragen zum Text!**

1. What does the killer think of the other people at the evening event?

____

____

2. Why are the police looking for Rob?

____

____

3. How do the police get into the suspect's flat?

____

____

4. How does Rob escape the killer's first attack?

____

____

"But why?" asked Rob.
"It should have been you and your dad that were killed on the coach that day."
"What coach?"
Rob was terrified, in pain and totally confused but knew he had to keep Will talking.

"The Manchester United coach massacre," said Will impatiently, as if the answer was obvious. He stopped walking, but pointed the knife at Rob. "It should have been you. My dad was all I had left. After he died they put me in care. I was moved from foster home to foster home. You have no idea of all the horrible things that were done to me. It's all your fault!"

"I…I was sick!" protested Rob. "I'm sorry for what happened to you, but no one knew what was going to happen that day. You and your dad were just very unlucky."

"Unlucky!" Will cackled manically, taking a step closer to Rob.

"It was you all this time?" asked Rob, desperate to keep him talking. "You killed all those people. Why?"

He just couldn't comprehend that his colleague and friend was capable of such horror.

"They let my father's killer get away," snarled Will. "It was bearable when one of those murderers was in jail. But then they let him go! Someone had to pay for my dad's death, especially that nurse bitch. She let my dad die! She said he had already gone, so she went to help someone else. But he hadn't! He couldn't have died; my dad wouldn't have left me like that."

Will approached Rob again with the knife, his eyes were unfocused and empty. Rob staggered back against the door. There was nowhere for him to go! Blood from his shoulder was running down his body and dripping onto the floor. His legs felt as if they were going to give way. In the distance Rob could hear the faint sound of police sirens. In his weakened state he knew he wouldn't be able to fight back.

Then Will brandished his knife and smiled hideously. "This is the end, Rob."

Suddenly Will groaned and dropped to his knees, revealing the elderly caretaker behind him, who was holding a broom. The caretaker hit Will around the head again. Will crumpled forwards onto the floor and his knife clattered away into the shadows. Rob and Will had been so focused on each other that neither of them had noticed the caretaker sneaking down the corridor behind them.

"Oh thank you," sobbed Rob in relief.

"Quickly, stop him!" shouted the caretaker.

The two men threw themselves on top of Will, pinning him down to the ground. Will's anger seemed to give him superhuman strength. The caretaker was breathing hard and Rob was injured. Rob knew they couldn't hold Will for long.

Suddenly they heard voices calling from somewhere in the stadium.

foster home	Pflegefamilie
to cackle	gackern, kichern
capable	fähig, imstande
state	Zustand
to brandish sth.	(herum)fuchteln mit
haze	Schleier, Nebel
unconsciousness	Bewusstlosigkeit

"Mr Anderson? Rob! This is the police. Can you hear us?"

"We're here! Help us, please!" Rob screamed in desperation.

He could feel himself growing weaker. He didn't know how long he could hold on.

"Stay with me, son," urged the caretaker as Will struggled wildly beneath them.

Rob heard the sound of running feet, and through a grey haze he saw the familiar face of Sergeant North approaching.

"Thank God," whispered Rob as he slipped into unconsciousness.

He knew he was safe.

FINAL TEST

Exercise 1: Adverbs. Ergänzen Sie die Adverbien!

1. Dave raised his eyebrows question ________________.
2. The woman leaned towards him secret ________________.
3. Judith was pushed back violent ____________________ into her house.
4. "Hello James," said Rob joke ________________. "Put any more murder victims in your column recent ______________."
5. "Of course I do," the man replied indignant ________________. "I rent the flat to him."
6. He pulled frantic ________________ at the handle.

Exercise 2: Irregular verbs. Ergänzen Sie die fehlenden Verbformen!

	Infinitive	Present Participle	Simple Past
1.	drive	______________	______________
2.	______________	writing	______________
3.	______________	waking	______________
4.	kneel	______________	______________
5.	______________	______________	crept

Exercise 3: Questions about the text. **Beantworten Sie die Fragen zum Text!**

1. Why do you think Will became a killer?

____

2. Why does Sergeant North like working with Detective Inspector McKay?

____

3. How did Rob feel when he discovered who the serial killer was?

____

4. How does the serial killer trick his way into Greg Summers' house?

____

Exercise 4: Was or were? **Ergänzen Sie die richtige Form!**

1. The opposition team had been playing well, but they ________ beginning to look tired.
2. Cameras flashed and questions ________ shouted.
3. There ________ no trace left on the knife.
4. The furniture in the room ________ basic.
5. Some ________ dribbling, most ________ asleep.
6. There ________ no mistaking the sound of footsteps this time.

Exercise 5: Compounds. Welche der folgenden Begriffe gehören zusammen? Ordnen Sie zu!

1. ☐ crime	a) home
2. ☐ witness	b) opera
3. ☐ notice	c) scene
4. ☐ foster	d) board
5. ☐ soap	e) statement

Exercise 6: Crossword puzzle. Lösen Sie das Kreuzworträtsel!

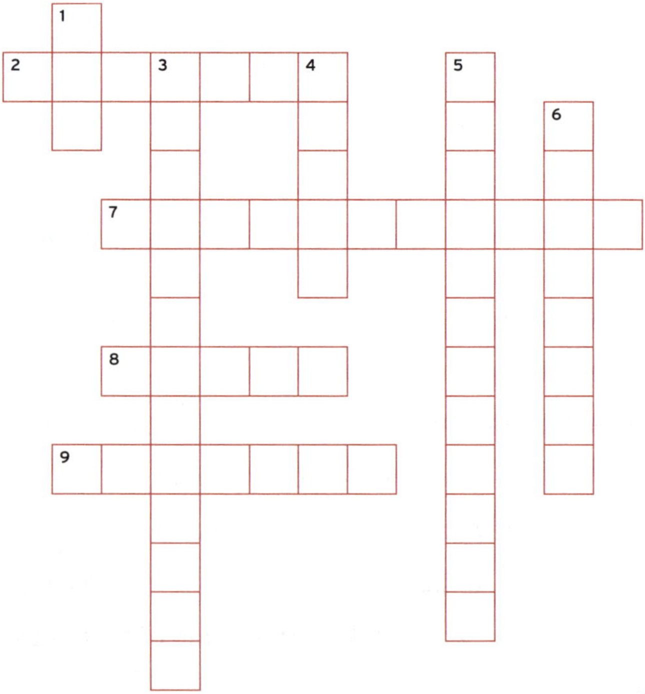

Across

2. a small area in a room that has been separated off

7. objects collected to remember a special event or place

8. a device that makes a loud warning sound

9. a large sports ground with rows of seats for spectators

Down

1. a building in which alcoholic drinks are served

3. a detailed inquiry into an incident to find out the truth

4. all

5. someone who has murdered several people

6. A murderer, thief or robber is a...

Exercise 7: Future forms. Setzen Sie die richtige Zukunftsform will, going oder going to ein!

1. My Dad was __________ take me.
2. Kevin __________ be expecting them.
3. They aren't __________ be happy.
4. Rob was __________ into work later.
5. Obviously we __________ read the article before it is published.
6. The visitor at the door was not __________ go away.

ANSWERS

Exercise 1: **1.** d **2.** a **3.** b **4.** c

Exercise 2: **1.** nearest **2.** old **3.** shabby **4.** busy **5.** great **6.** Red

Exercise 3: **1.** won't **2.** don't **3.**That's **4.** You're **5.** wasn't **6.** can't

Exercise 4: **Across:** manager, net, player, stadium
Down: match, goalkeeper, whistle, referee, defender, striker

Exercise 5: **1.** heard, heard **2.** took, taken **3.** went, gone **4.** knew, known **5.** was/were, been

Exercise 6: **1.** false **2.** true **3.** true **4.** false **5.** false

Exercise 7: **1.** instantly **2.** survived **3.** gun **4.** Minister **5.** country

Exercise 8: **1.** see **2.** had seen **3.** come **4.** imagining **5.** watched **6.** turned

Exercise 9: **1.** passengers **2.** armchair **3.** reliable **4.** interrupt **5.** encounter **6.** fortnight

Exercise 10: **1.** were expecting **2.** passes **3.** runs **4.** is looking **5.** approaches

Exercise 11: **1.** b **2.** a **3.** d **4.** e **5.** c

Exercise 12: **1.** busily **2.** tired **3.** loudly **4.** cold **5.** carefully

Exercise 13: **1.** yawned **2.** city centre **3.** stop **4.** sirens **5.** pavement

Exercise 14: **1.** one **2.** to **3.** so **4.** seen **5.** see **6.** too

Exercise 15:

1 G	2 L	3 O	4 V	5 E	6 S	7 O	8 B
22 R	23 E	24 A	25 M	26 A	27 G	28 A	9 R
21 C	36 Y	37 O	38 U	39 T	40 H	29 Z	10 E
20 S	35 T	34 P	33 M	32 E	31 N	30 I	11 A
19 S	18 E	17 L	16 E	15 M	14 O	13 H	12 T

Exercise 16: **1.** d **2.** e **3.** b **4.** a **5.** c
Exercise 17: **1.** him **2.** his **3.** She **4.** her **5.** you **6.** He
Exercise 18: **1.** Rob's computer **2.** the three men's editor **3.** the girls' bottoms **4.** Rob and Will's conversation
5. James's laugh
Exercise 19: **1.** have been killed **2.** is interviewing **3.** will strike
4. was trying **5.** struck
Exercise 20: **1.** The police have asked Rob to write an article for them.
2. Greg Summers was wearing a Manchester United football shirt when he was killed, and Fans United has a lot of readers who may have some information.
3. DI McKay supports Newcastle United; Sergeant North supports Manchester United.
4. Greg Summers was a taxi driver.
Exercise 21: **1.** normal **2.** clean **3.** boring **4.** busy
Exercise 22: **1.** pavement **2.** stubble **3.** familiar **4.** tangled
5. pocket **6.** pursuer **7.** headphones **8.** anger
Lösung: murderer
Exercise 23: **1.** Susan and Rob don't go out together once a week.
2. The restaurant wasn't quiet.
3. They didn't listen to the Indian music.
4. Susan and Rob aren't in love.
5. Susan isn't going into work early tomorrow.
Exercise 24: **1.** I still thought (think) **2.** an (a) homeless man
3. which (who/whom) **4.** their (they're)
5. much (many) **6.** persons (people)
Exercise 25: **1.** stranger, strangest **2.** angry, angriest
3. low, lower **4.** happier, happiest **5.** more comfortable, most comfortable
Exercise 26: **1.** on **2.** out **3.** into **4.** opposite **5.** at
Exercise 27: **Across: 1.** photograph **5.** officer **7.** article
Down: 2. blood **3.** magazine **4.** coat **6.** relax
Exercise 28: **1.** noon **2.** driveway **3.** garage **4.** boot **5.** lock **6.** lawn

Exercise 29: **1.** Max cursed as he entered the house.
2. There was no sign of the dogs.
3. It was a relatively warm autumn day.
4. He opened the glass patio doors.

Exercise 30: **1.** bitterly **2.** ugly **3.** sharply **4.** coldly **5.** manically

Exercise 31: **1.** c **2.** a **3.** d **4.** e **5.** b

Exercise 32: **1.** watching **2.** replied **3.** stood **4.** getting **5.** make

Exercise 33: **1.** "Why would I agree to visit your mother **when** I know I have to work?"
2. The screensaver disappeared **as** he touched the keyboard.
3. "My mum has specially bought a leg of lamb to roast **and** Auntie Elsa is coming to visit as well."
4. She looked hurt **but** stopped talking.

Exercise 34: **1.** „Was geht hier vor?" fragte er. „Es muss ein Zufall sein."
2. Rob ließ die Zeitschrift zu Boden fallen.
3. Ein Mordopfer war nicht weit von seiner Wohnung gefunden worden.
4. „Versprich mir, vorsichtig zu sein."

Exercise 35: **1.** c **2.** a **3.** a **4.** b

Exercise 36: **1.** notebook **2.** taxi **3.** prison **4.** files **5.** motive

Exercise 37: **1.** He laid his head in his hands. **2.** They lived in the Greater Manchester area. **3.** "It can't be him," said Sergeant North. **4.** "I'll go and find her now."

Exercise 38: **1.** keeping **2.** turned **3.** was standing **4.** was wearing **5.** smiled **6.** shook

Exercise 39: **Across: 2.** relatives **5.** local **6.** caretaker **8.** judge **9.** crowd
Down: 1. competition **3.** taxi **4.** Portugal **7.** entrance **10.** camera

Exercise 40: **1.** collected **2.** put **3.** had put on **4.** (had) finished **5.** hadn't taken **6.** filled

Exercise 41: **1.** unease, uneasily **2.** desperation, desperately **3.** anger, angrily **4.** violence, violently **5.** strangeness, strangely

Exercise 42: **1.** doesn't he **2.** didn't they **3.** isn't she **4.** had he **5.** will he

Exercise 43: **1.** difficult **2.** know **3.** knew **4.** violent **5.** something **6.** death

Exercise 44: our, we, It, he, his, We, it, your, our, it

Exercise 45: **1.** coach **2.** eavesdrop **3.** hospital **4.** nurse **5.** suspicious **6.** brainwave **7.** thread **8.** search engine **9.** nonsense **10.** recruit **11.** heroine
Lösung: coincidence

Exercise 46: **1.** a **2.** b **3.** b **4.** a **5.** b

Exercise 47: **1.** comfort **2.** hidden **3.** secret **4.** revenge **5.** practised

Exercise 48: **1.** said **2.** reaching **3.** happened **4.** heard **5.** to evacuate **6.** ran

Exercise 49: **1.** d **2.** e **3.** a **4.** c **5.** b

Exercise 50: Abends trafen sich Rob und Dave in ihrem Lieblingspub in South Manchester, dem Didsbury Arms, um sich das Mittwochabendsspiel anzusehen. Manchester United spielte diesmal in München. Rob kam mit zwei Gläsern/Pints Bier und ein paar Päckchen Erdnüssen zurück von der Bar.

Exercise 51: **Across: 1.** colleague **3.** canteen **5.** guffaw **6.** sad **7.** couple **10.** student
Down: 2. announcement **4.** now **6.** stress **8.** peanuts **9.** exact

Exercise 52: **1.** his **2.** her **3.** their **4.** my **5.** our

Exercise 53: **1.** to **2.** of **3.** for **4.** out **5.** at

Exercise 54: **1.** b **2.** c **3.** b **4.** a **5.** a

Exercise 55: **1.** his hatred was burning inside him **2.** He smiled to himself. **3.** He was so bored **4.** The noise of the party

Exercise 56: **1.** d **2.** c **3.** e **4.** a **5.** b

Exercise 57: **1.** furniture (furnitures) **2.** caught (catched) **3.** Sergeant North's (Sergeant Norths) **4.** quickly (quick) **5.** fell (felt) **6.** looked (looking)

Exercise 58:

1 O	2 B	3 E	4 S	5 E	6 M	7 B	8 A
22 U	23 M	24 P	25 S	26 I	27 G	28 H	9 R
21 B	36 Q	37 U	38 I	39 R	40 Y	29 E	10 R
20 E	35 N	34 E	33 N	32 I	31 O	30 R	11 A
19 S	18 O	17 O	16 G	15 N	14 I	13 S	12 S

Exercise 59: **1.** ago **2.** since **3.** before **4.** for **5.** yesterday

Exercise 60: **1.** shall **2.** must **3.** will **4.** could **5.** may

Exercise 61: **1.** The killer thinks the other people are idiots, stupid and weak.

2. There is a photograph of Rob on the killer's wall.

3. The suspect's landlord lives next door and unlocks the door for them.

4. Rob lurches to one side and the killer falls down the stairs.

FINAL TEST

Exercise 1: **1.** questioningly **2.** secretively **3.** violently **4.** jokingly, recently **5.** indignantly **6.** frantically

Exercise 2: **1.** driving, drove **2.** write, wrote **3.** wake, woke **4.** kneeling, kneeled/knelt, **5.** creep, creeping

Exercise 3: **1.** Will wanted revenge for his father's death and the horrible things that were done to him in child care. He began to kill when Jared Cook was released from prison.

2. Detective Inspector McKay had really looked after Sergeant North since he joined the police force. He understands that everyone has to learn and he is always there to give advice.

3. Rob felt shocked and afraid. He was also confused as he couldn't understand how someone he thought was a friend could do such terrible things.

4. The killer pretends to be delivering a heavy box to Greg Summers.

Exercise 4: **1.** were **2.** were **3.** was **4.** was **5.** were, were **6.** was

Exercise 5: **1.** c **2.** e **3.** d **4.** a **5.** b

Exercise 6: **Across: 2.** cubicle **7.** memorabilia **8.** siren **9.** stadium

Down: 1. pub **3.** investigation **4.** every **5.** serial killer **6.** criminal

Exercise 7: **1.** going to **2.** will **3.** going to **4.** going **5.** will **6.** going to

GLOSSARY

ϟ = umgangssprachlich
pl = Plural

absent-mindedly	geistesabwesend
accusingly	vorwurfsvoll
acquaintance	Bekannte(r)
admittedly	zugegebenermaßen
agony	heftige Schmerzen
aimlessly	ziellos
alert	Alarm
anniversary	Jahrestag
anxious(ly)	besorgt
to appeal for information	um Hinweise bitten
to appreciate sth.	etw. zu schätzen wissen
approval	Zustimmung, Freigabe
assailant	Angreifer(in)
assigned	zugewiesen
available	verfügbar
awful	furchtbar, schrecklich
awkward(ly)	unangenehm, peinlich
backyard	Hinterhof
balaclava	Sturmhaube
balding	eine Glatze bekommen
to be beyond reproach	über jeden Tadel erhaben sein
to be in charge of sth.	befehlen, am Drücker sitzen
ϟ to be miles away	mit den Gedanken ganz woanders sein
bemused	verwirrt, verständnislos

benefit	Vorteil, Vorzug
to be on edge	nervös sein
to be on the verge of sth.	kurz vor etw. stehen
to be signed	unter Vertrag genommen werden
to be supposed to do sth.	etw. tun sollen
to betray sb.	jmd. verraten
biased	*hier*: parteiisch
ϟ bigwig	ϟ hohes Tier
blade	Klinge
to blare	heulen, dröhnen
to blend into sth.	verschmelzen mit
blurred	verschwommen
to blush	erröten
to boil	kochen
bolt upright	kerzengerade
booming	dröhnend
bouncer	Türsteher
to bound	springen
bow	Verbeugung
to brandish sth.	(herum)fuchteln mit
ϟ brainwave	Geistesblitz
to bring sb. in	jmd. zur Vernehmung bringen
brooding	grüblerisch
to burp	rülpsen
to burst (burst, burst)	bersten, herausbrechen
bustling	belebt, geschäftig
to butcher sb.	jmd. abschlachten
to buzz with sth.	erfüllt sein mit
by chance	zufällig
to cackle	gackern, kichern
campaigner	Aktivist(in), Kämpfer(in)
capable	fähig, imstande
to capture	einfangen
care home	Pflegeheim
case	Fall
to catch one's eye	jmd. ins Auge fallen
to catch sb. off guard	jmd. überrumpeln

CCTV footage	Überwachungsvideo(s)
chairman	Vorsitzender
⚡ chap	⚡ Typ, Kerl
to charge with criminal damage and assault	anklagen wegen Sachbeschädigung und Körperverletzung
chart	Diagramm, Grafik
cheeky	frech, unverschämt
to cheer	jubeln
cheerful(ly)	gut gelaunt, fröhlich
cheers	Prost
to chuckle	kichern
to circulate sth.	etw. herumgeben, in Umlauf bringen
to claim	behaupten
to clatter	klappern, poltern
to clear one's throat	sich räuspern
to clench one's fists	die Fäuste ballen
close	*hier*: knapp
clue	Hinweis
coincidence	Zufall
cold case squad	Dezernat für ungeklärte Fälle
to collapse	zusammenbrechen
column	Kolumne
commotion	Tumult, Unruhe
communal	gemeinschaftlich
to concede	eingestehen, zugeben
concerned	besorgt
concrete	Beton
confession	Geständnis
to confirm	bestätigen
conscious	bei Bewusstsein
to consult sth.	*hier*: nachsehen/nachschlagen in
corpse	Leiche
cosy	heimelig, gemütlich
to cower	kauern, sich ducken
creased	zerknittert
credits *pl*	*hier*: Abspann
crime scene	Tatort

crisps *pl*	Kartoffelchips
cubicle	Kabine
to curse	fluchen
debris	Abfälle, Überbleibsel
defaced	verunstaltet
defender	Verteidiger
demanding	anstrengend, anspruchsvoll
deserted	verlassen
detached	distanziert, unbeteiligt
detached house	freistehendes Haus
ϟ to die	*hier*: ausgehen
to dig (dug, dug)	*hier*: wühlen, suchen
dimly	dunkel, schwach
to discard	ablegen, fallen lassen
dishevelled	unordentlich, ungepflegt
distinctive	unverwechselbar
to distract	ablenken
disturbing	verstörend, beunruhigend
divorce	Scheidung
ϟ dodgy	zweifelhaft, riskant
to draw a blank	kein Glück haben, eine Niete ziehen
to draw to a close	sich dem Ende zuneigen
dressing gown	Bademantel
to dribble	sabbern
dusk	Abenddämmerung
eager(ly)	begierig, eifrig
earnestly	ernst(haft)
to eavesdrop	(be)lauschen
to edge backwards	sich langsam rückwärts bewegen
editor	Redakteur(in)
elderly	ältere(r), ältlich
embroidered	gestickt
encounter	Begegnung
encouragingly	aufmunternd
to erase	auslöschen, ausradieren
evidence	Beweis(e)
façade	Fassade, Anschein

face like thunder	finstere Miene
ϟ to fancy sth.	auf etw. Lust haben, etw. wollen
to fan out	ausschwärmen
far-fetched	weit hergeholt
feature	großer Artikel
ϟ fella	ϟ Typ
to fiddle	herumspielen
fierce	heftig, erbittert
file	Akte
filthy	dreckig
to flicker	flackern
flick knife	Klappmesser
to flinch	zusammenzucken
flurry of activity	Hektik
to follow up on sth.	etw. weiterverfolgen, einer Sache nachgehen
fool	Idiot
to force	zwingen
form	Formular
fortnight	vierzehn Tage
foster home	Pflegefamilie
frantically	panisch
fringe	*hier*: Pony
fruitless	erfolglos
to fume	vor Wut schäumen
fuss	Getue, Wirbel
gaping	klaffend
to get away with sth.	mit etw. durchkommen
to get hold of sth.	*hier*: herankommen an
to get the better of sb.	über jmd. die Oberhand gewinnen
to glance	blicken
glare	wütender Blick
to gleam	funkeln, glitzern
to glint	glitzern
to glisten	(feucht) glänzen
gloomy	düster, trostlos
glued	festgeklebt

ϟ Good grief!	Du meine Güte!
goosebumps *pl*	Gänsehaut
Great Dane	Deutsche Dogge
grim(ly)	grimmig, finster
to groan	(auf)stöhnen
to growl	knurren
guffaw	schallendes Gelächter
gunman	Bewaffneter
hatred	Hass
ϟ to have a (bit of a) soft spot for sb.	eine (kleine) Schwäche für jmd. haben
ϟ to have a natter	quatschen
haze	Schleier, Nebel
to head (back)	(zurück)eilen
headline	Schlagzeile
heated argument	hitziger/heftiger Streit
heroine	Heldin
to hitch up	hochziehen
hoarse	heiser
homeless	obdachlos
hospitality suite	Besucherlounge, VIP-Lounge
hum	Brummen, Knattern
humiliating	demütigend
ϟ hun (honey)	Schatz
to hurl sth.	etw. schleudern
to illuminate	erleuchten
imagination	Fantasie, Vorstellungskraft
to imply sth.	etw. andeuten
in awe	bewundernd
incident	Vorfall, Zwischenfall
incident room	Einsatzzentrale
indignantly	entrüstet, aufgebracht
indulgent	nachsichtig, milde
initial	erste(r,s), anfänglich
injured	verletzt
to insist	bestehen auf
insistent	hartnäckig

instrumental	entscheidend
invincible	unbesiegbar
invisible	unsichtbar
irritating	ärgerlich
to jail	inhaftieren, einsperren
jaw	Kiefer
to jolt awake	aus dem Schlaf hochschrecken
justice	Gerechtigkeit
to keep a straight face	ernst bleiben, sich das Lachen verkneifen
kennel	Zwinger
kerb	Bordstein
to kick in	anspringen, sich einschalten
to label	beschriften, betiteln
landline	Festnetz
landlord	Vermieter
to launch oneself at sb.	sich auf jmd. stürzen
lead	Spur, Hinweis
to leaf through sth.	etw. durchblättern
ϟ to leap (leapt, leapt) out	*hier*: hervorstechen, auffallen
to leap to conclusions	voreilige Schlüsse ziehen
line	*hier*: Kollektion
line of enquiry	Untersuchungsrichtung
litter	Müll
to lurch	torkeln
to lose one's bearings	die Orientierung verlieren
to make sb. jump	jmd. zusammenzucken lassen
Managing Director	Geschäftsführer(in)
maniac	Wahnsinniger, Irrer
marshal	*hier*: Ordner, Platzwart
massive	riesig
ϟ mate	ϟ Kumpel
maze	Labyrinth
memorabilia *pl*	Souvenirs
to mingle	sich mischen
mischievous(ly)	verschmitzt, schelmisch
miserable	unglücklich, griesgrämig

to moan	stöhnen
momentum	Schwung, Wucht
to mow	mähen
muffled	gedämpft
mute	stumm
mutilated	verstümmelt
⚡ mutt	⚡ Köter
to mutter	murmeln
nagging	nörgelnd
notable	berühmt, bekannt
notoriously	notorisch, bekannt für
obese	fettleibig
to obliterate	auslöschen, tilgen
odd	einzeln, gelegentlich; seltsam, komisch
off-duty	nicht im Dienst
opponent	Gegner(in), Widersacher(in)
oppressive	(er)drückend
outline	Umriss
to over-react	überreagieren
⚡ over the top	übertrieben
to overwhelm	überwältigen, überschwemmen
to pace	auf und ab gehen
to pad	tappen, trotten
to pant	keuchen, schnaufen
to pass in a blur	wie im Flug vergehen
patio	Terrasse
patrol car	Streifenwagen
pattern	Muster, Schema
to peer	spähen, schauen
to persist	andauern, fortbestehen
⚡ pest	⚡ Nervensäge, Plage
petulantly	verdrossen
physical	körperlich
to pierce	durchbrechen
⚡ pig	⚡ Bulle
pile	Stapel

pint	Pint (0,568 l)
pitch	Spielfeld, Platz
plain	einfach, unscheinbar
plumber	Klemptner(in)
to plunge into	(ein)tauchen in
to poke out	hervorgucken
posh	vornehm, piekfein
to pound	hämmern
to pour sth.	etw. einschenken
to pray	beten
to predict sth.	etw. vorhersagen
preoccupied	besorgt, nachdenklich
preparation	Vorbereitung
to prevent sb. from doing sth.	jmd. daran hindern, etw. zu tun
prime suspect	Hauptverdächtige(r)
private	*hier*: verschlossen, introvertiert
proper	anständig, richtig
prospect	Aussicht
to provide	liefern, bereitstellen
to publish	veröffentlichen
to purse one's lips	den Mund verziehen
to put up with sth.	etw. aushalten, etw. ertragen
puzzle	Rätsel
puzzled	verwirrt
ϟ racket	Krach, Lärm
radio	*hier*: Funk
ragged	ausgefranst, zerrissen
random	zufällig
razor-sharp	rasiermesserscharf
reassuringly	beruhigend
ϟ to reckon	denken, glauben
ϟ ref (referee)	ϟ Schiri
to release	freilassen
to release sb. on bail	jmd. gegen Kaution freilassen
reliable	verlässlich
relief	Erleichterung

to relive	(im Geiste) noch einmal erleben
remotely	entfernt
renewed purpose	neuer Elan
to restrain sb.	jmd. bändigen
to retire	in Rente gehen
to retrieve	zurückholen
to rev the engine	den Motor aufheulen lassen
to roar	brüllen, (auf)heulen
robe	Richterrobe
rootless	heimatlos, entwurzelt
roundabout	Kreisverkehr
rowdy	rüpelhaft, wild
to rummage	kramen, wühlen
to run an article	einen Artikel bringen
savage	brutal, wild
sb.'s heart sinks	jmd. rutscht das Herz in die Hose
sb.'s mind is whirling	jmd. schwirrt der Kopf
scornfully	verächtlich
to scribble	(hin)kritzeln
scuffling	raufend
ϟ scum	Abschaum
sensible	vernünftig
serial killer	Serienmörder(in)
to settle down	es sich bequem machen
severe	schwer, ernsthaft
shaft	Strahl
shaken	erschüttert, aufgewühlt
to shatter	zerbrechen, zersplittern
to shift one's weight	sein Gewicht verlagern
to shriek	kreischen
to shrug	die Schultern zucken
sickening thump	entsetzlicher Knall
sinister	unheilvoll, unheimlich
to sleep (slept, slept) soundly	tief und fest schlafen
to slump	zusammensinken
smart	*hier*: schick

ϟ snap	Schnappschuss
to snap	blaffen
to snarl	(wütend) knurren
to snort	schnauben, prusten
to sob	schluchzen
sociable	gesellig
solicitor	Anwalt/Anwältin
soothing	beruhigend, entspannend
to sparkle	glitzern
stable	Stall
to stab to death	erstechen
stadium	Stadion
to stagger	torkeln, wanken
stained	verfärbt, befleckt
to stalk out	hinausmarschieren
stand	Zuschauertribüne
staple	Heftklammer
to startle sb.	jmd. aufschrecken, jmd. erschrecken
state	Zustand
stationery	Schreibwaren
to steady sth.	etw. stabilisieren
to stir up	entfachen, aufwirbeln
to stoke	anfachen
stooped	altersgebeugt
to stride (strode, –)	schreiten
to strike (struck, struck)	zuschlagen, angreifen
striker	Stürmer
stubble	Bartstoppeln
subdued	gedämpft, düster
subtle	*hier*: klein; subtil
surveillance	Überwachung
to survey	überblicken
suspicious(ly)	verdächtig
to swap	wechseln, tauschen
swiftly	schnell
ϟ swig	Schluck
sympathetic(ally)	verständnisvoll

tackle	Angriff, Tackling
tainted evidence	fingierte/nicht verwertbare Beweise
to tap	(leicht) klopfen
tap	Wasserhahn
target	Ziel
↯ tatty	schäbig, abgewetzt
to taunt	verspotten, herausfordern
to tease	necken, aufziehen
temple	*hier*: Schläfe; Tempel
to tense	(sich) anspannen
tentative	vorläufig, provisorisch
terraced house	Reihenhaus
terrified	total verängstigt
↯ The cheek!	So eine Frechheit!
the implication was that...	man konnte daraus schließen, dass ...
thread	Faden
threatening(ly)	drohend
to throw the first punch	den ersten Schlag austeilen
to thrust (thrust, thrust)	stoßen
thug	Schlägertyp
to toss sth.	werfen, schleudern
tracksuit bottoms *pl*	Jogginghosen
treat	*hier*: Aufmerksamkeit, Geschenk
tree-lined	von Bäumen gesäumt
trespassing	unbefugtes Betreten
trial	Gerichtsverfahren
trickle	Tropfen, Rinnsal
trolley	Rollwagen
tucked	geklemmt, gesteckt
to turn on sb.	sich gegen jmd. wenden, auf jmd. losgehen
to twirl	drehen
unbearable	unerträglich
unconsciousness	Bewusstlosigkeit
unintelligible	unverständlich
unsettling	beunruhigend

unsuspecting	ahnungslos, nichts ahnend
to vent	ablassen, (sich) Luft machen
verdict	Urteil
vice-like	wie ein Schraubstock
viciously	boshaft, gemein
victim	Opfer
to wag	wedeln
to wave	winken
weary	müde, erschöpft
Well, well!	Na, sowas! Na, sieh mal einer an!
well-groomed	gepflegt
to whimper	wimmern
ϟ to whizz past	vorbeirasen
ϟ Whoopsie!	ϟ Uups!
willpower	Willenskraft
to wink	zwinkern
witness statement	Zeugenaussage
to wobble	schwanken, wackeln
workload	Arbeitsbelastung
workmate	Arbeitskollege/-kollegin
worktop	Arbeitsfläche
ϟ worth a shot	einen Versuch wert
to wrack sth.	etw. erschüttern
wryly	trocken, ironisch
to yell	brüllen, schreien
yelp	Kleffen, Gebell
ϟ Yuck!	Igitt!

LIST OF EXERCISES

Final Test

Compact Lernkrimis auch in Spanisch, Französisch, Italienisch, Deutsch und Schwedisch erhältlich.

Compact Lernkrimi
Classic

A1

A2

B1

Art and Ashes
ISBN 978-3-8174-8970-1

Cook and Kill
ISBN 978-3-8174-8969-5

Das Rätsel der Mumie
ISBN 978-3-8174-7304-5

Deadly Mistake
ISBN 978-3-8174-8259-7

Death Wasn't the Deal
ISBN 978-3-8174-8968-8

Der Rächer von Canterbury
ISBN 978-3-8174-7662-6

Der rote Nebel
ISBN 978-3-8174-7574-2

Ein fast perfekter Coup
ISBN 978-3-8174-7568-1

Game Over in Soho
ISBN 978-3-8174-7878-1

Hunting the Vampire
ISBN 978-3-8174-7305-2

Im Schatten des Towers
ISBN 978-3-8174-7687-9

Komplott unter Palmen
ISBN 978-3-8174-7571-1

Schüsse im Nebel
ISBN 978-3-8174-7763-0

Tod eines Dandys
ISBN 978-3-8174-7660-2

Toxic Testament
ISBN 978-3-8174-7879-8

American English

Tod im Grand Canyon
ISBN 978-3-8174-7572-8

Sammelband 3 in 1 (B1/B2)

Inspector Hudson Investigates
ISBN 978-3-8174-7625-1

London Crime Time
ISBN 978-3-8174-7787-6

B2

Bloody Diamonds
ISBN 978-3-8174-8971-8

Das geheimnisvolle Gemälde
ISBN 978-3-8174-7306-9

Der Seelenjäger
ISBN 978-3-8174-7581-0

Der unheimliche Ritter
ISBN 978-3-8174-7661-9

Die Rache des Lords
ISBN 978-3-8174-7663-3

Die Spur des Höllenhundes
ISBN 978-3-8174-7307-6

Diebstahl im Morgengrauen
ISBN 978-3-8174-7638-1

Lady Mayfairs Rache
ISBN 978-3-8174-7815-6

Nobody Dies Twice
ISBN 978-3-8174-8972-5

Schatten der Vergangenheit
ISBN 978-3-8174-7570-4

Business English

Das letzte Roulette
ISBN 978-3-8174-7609-1

Der 25-Millionen-Coup
ISBN 978-3-8174-7659-6

Schmierige Geschäfte
ISBN 978-3-8174-7658-9

Teuflische Intrigen
ISBN 978-3-8174-7608-4

C1/C2

A Scottish Murder Mystery
ISBN 978-3-8174-8379-2

Compact Lernkrimi
Kurzkrimis

Compact Lernkrimi
Lernthriller

Compact Lernkrimi Kurzkrimis	Compact Lernkrimi Lernthriller	
		A1
Blood and Breakfast ISBN 978-3-8174-7760-9 **Deadly Business** ISBN 978-3-8174-9215-2 **It Was Murder, My Lord** ISBN 978-3-8174-7734-0 **Last Exit Waterloo Bridge** ISBN 978-3-8174-7733-3 **Murder at Teatime** ISBN 978-3-8174-7839-2 **<u>Sammelband 10 in 1 (A2/B1)</u>** **Murderous Collection** ISBN 978-3-8174-8967-1		A2
Bullets over Bristol ISBN 978-3-8174-8544-4 **Death Comes Knocking** ISBN 978-3-8174-7945-0 **<u>American Business English</u>** **Murderous Network** ISBN 978-3-8174-9312-8	**Massacre United** ISBN 978-3-8174-9319-7 **<u>American English</u>** **Faceless Killer** ISBN 978-3-8174-8856-8	B1
	In Terror ISBN 978-3-8174-8857-5	B2
		C1/C2

Compact Lernkrimi
Rätselblock

Compact Lernkrimi
Hörbuch

A1		
A2	**The Art of Crime** ISBN 978-3-8174-9155-1	**A Shot in the Night** ISBN 978-3-8174-8202-3 **Death Wish** ISBN 978-3-8174-8204-7 **The Butterworth Mystery** ISBN 978-3-8174-8203-0
B1	**A Deadly Puzzle** ISBN 978-3-8174-8832-2	**Bloody Revenge** ISBN 978-3-8174-8860-5 **Danger at King's Cross** ISBN 978-3-8174-7673-2 **The Thames Murderer** ISBN 978-3-8174-7674-9
B2		**Blutige Erbschaft** ISBN 978-3-8174-7676-3 **Die Intrigantin** ISBN 978-3-8174-7675-6 **Business English** **Crime & Company** ISBN 978-3-8174-8976-3 **Murder at the Office** ISBN 978-3-8174-7747-0
C1/C2		

Compact Lernkrimi
Audio-Learning

Compact Lernkrimi
Sprachkurs

Compact Lernkrimi Audio-Learning	Compact Lernkrimi Sprachkurs	
	Englisch für Anfänger (A1/A2) ISBN 978-3-8174-7784-5	A1
Verschollen im Dartmoor ISBN 978-3-8174-7796-8		A2
Totenstille im Hyde Park ISBN 978-3-8174-7797-5		B1
		B2
		C1/C2